Their Family Blessing

Lorraine Beatty

S0-AGX-453

Recycling programs
for this product may
not exist in your area.

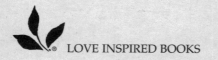 LOVE INSPIRED BOOKS

ISBN-13: 978-1-335-53901-4

Their Family Blessing

www.Harlequin.com

Printed in U.S.A.

Judge not, and ye shall not be judged:
condemn not, and ye shall not be condemned:
forgive, and ye shall be forgiven.
—*Luke* 6:37

To my precious daughters-in-law,
Robin and Cindy, who have made my sons happy
all these years. You are a blessing to all of us.

Chapter One

The office was exactly what widow Carly Porter Hughes had expected from a small-town attorney. Wood paneling, thick carpets, massive desk and walls lined with legal books. It had been designed to instill trust and confidence in those who entered, none of which she was feeling at the moment. Nathan Holt came around his desk, greeting her with a smile and a firm handshake before smiling down at her six-year-old daughter, Ella.

Carly hugged Ella close to her side. "I hope you don't mind me bringing her along. I had no one to leave her with."

"Certainly not. In fact, I have some books over here she can look at while we talk business."

With Ella settled in, Carly took a seat in front of the desk, smoothed the front of her gray skirt, then clasped her hands tightly in her lap. The reading of the will. The whole situation seemed surreal. She never expected to be back in Hastings, Mississippi, and she certainly hadn't expected to inherit anything from her father. They hadn't spoken in years. Mostly she resented the demand for her presence at the reading.

Carly swallowed past the tightness in her throat. All she wanted to do was get through this ordeal and head back to Atlanta, where she belonged. "Can we get started, Mr. Holt? I'm anxious to get back home."

Holt nodded slowly. "I understand, but we're waiting for the other beneficiary to arrive. He should be here any moment."

"Other beneficiary?" Who in the world could he be talking about? She had no siblings, and only a very distant cousin she'd never even met. She started to ask who it was when the door opened behind her and Holt stood, a welcoming smile on his round face.

"Ah, there you are. Have a seat, Mr. Bridges, and we'll get started."

Carly's heart skipped a beat. No. It couldn't be. She turned her head to the side and her gaze traveled up the long length of the man who had entered. Her gaze collided with his and her mind hiccupped. Mackenzie Bridges. The last person on earth she wanted to see.

He held her gaze, a hint of amusement lifting one side of his mouth. "Hello, Carly." He took the seat beside her and crossed his long legs.

It took her longer than it should have to find her voice. Mack had changed. He'd be thirty-four now, two years older than her, and the years had been very kind to him. The tall slender boy she remembered had grown into a very handsome man. His six-foot frame had developed a pair of broad shoulders that spoke of his strength. His dark brown hair, once so long and careless, was now trimmed neatly, wavy enough so it invited a woman to run her fingers through it. His sky blue eyes still held a perpetual sparkle, and his crooked smile was still very much in evidence and hadn't lost any of its charm. "You're the other beneficiary?"

"It appears so."

She should have known. Her father had always loved Mack, his surrogate son, more than her.

Holt opened the file and Mack leaned forward, looking over at Ella. "Yours?"

"Yes." Carly tried to not look at him, but he was still very hard to ignore. Dressed in dark slacks and a pale blue shirt, he looked professional. Not like the jeans-and-T-shirt-wearing boy she remembered. Pushing her hair behind her ear, she refocused. She wanted to get through the reading and go home. Holt began explaining about the unusual nature of the will, which sent a small frisson of concern along her nerves.

"To my daughter, Carly Porter Hughes, I leave the Longleaf Lodge and all its contents."

She breathed a sigh of relief. This was the first light at the end of the dark financial tunnel she'd been in for the last few years. Things had been hard enough after her husband had died, but the addition of Ella's surgery had only made things worse.

"To my dear friend, Mackenzie Scott Bridges, I leave all the land on which Longleaf Lodge sits, including the cabins, canoe livery, pool and campgrounds."

Mack rubbed his forehead. "This doesn't make any sense. Why not divide it up equally between us?"

Holt peered over his glasses. "There's more."

He read a long passage of legalese that left Carly more confused than ever. "I'm sorry, but could you just spell it out for me."

The attorney sighed, removed his glasses and then leaned back in his chair. "Basically it comes down to this. Neither of you can sell your portion of the estate unless both agree. You are required to live at the lodge for the next two months, reopen the business and run it for the duration of this agreement. At the end of that time if you haven't agreed to either keep the estate and continue to run it jointly or mutually agreed to sell, then the estate will be put up for auction and the proceeds given to charity."

Carly's mind was reeling. "Can he do this? We either follow his dictates or we get nothing?"

"I'm afraid so. I understand this is an unusual situation, but I assure you it's all legal. Of course, if you both agree to sell, we can start that process right now."

"Yes. I want to sell."

Mack gave her an incredulous look. "No. Wade loved that lodge. He wouldn't want us to sell out."

Holt nodded. "Then until you are in agreement, you'll be required to follow your father's requirements."

Carly's pulse raced and heat crawled up her neck. "This is absurd. Isn't there anything you can do?" The pleading in her voice was embarrassing.

"Nothing. It's in your hands now. However, I'll be here to help in any way with advice, and there's an account set up for you to use to make any repairs and small upgrades to the estate."

Her concern slid into fear. "Repairs? What kind of condition is the lodge in?"

Holt stood, signaling the meeting was over. "The lodge has been closed for the last two months. Your father was too sick to manage the place, and the Thompsons, who have managed the business for thirty years, couldn't run it alone. But it was your father's greatest desire to see the lodge up and running again."

Of course it was. It was the only thing Wade Porter ever cared about, certainly not his wife and daughter. Carly stood and held out her hand to Ella. "Let's go, sweetie. I'm all done."

She was keenly aware of Mack following her out into the reception area. The scent of his spicy aftershave made him hard to ignore.

"Uncle Mack. Are you rich?"

A little blond-haired girl about Ella's age jumped up and hurried toward Mack.

Carly spun and looked at Mack. He returned the child's hug with a wide smile. The look of affection in his blue eyes made one thing clear. He loved the little girl.

"It's not polite to speak about money, but no, I'm not. I told you this wasn't about money."

What did he mean by that? Was he making a not-too-subtle dig at her request to sell the estate? It probably had sounded mercenary, but she had a good reason. What did he hope to get out of this bequest?

He met her gaze, and one corner of his mouth arched as if amused. "This is my niece. Lucy, this is an old— This is Mr. Wade's daughter, Miss Carly, and her daughter, Ella."

Despite her roiling emotions, she couldn't resist the sweet smile on Lucy's face. "Hello, Lucy. Is she Valerie's child?"

"Yes." His expression turned serious. "We need to talk. Why don't we meet at the lodge in an hour, get settled in and see what we can work out?"

"I'm not staying at the lodge."

Mack lowered his voice and pinned her with his steely blue gaze. "I believe Mr. Holt stated that staying at the lodge was one of the conditions of the will. Would you like to double-check with him? Or are you ready to let your dad's estate go up for auction tomorrow?"

She hated being forced to do things. How like her dad to die and leave a complicated mess behind. She wanted no part of it. But if she had any chance of inheriting even a small sum, she had to go along. Her only hope was to convince Mack to sell his portion, then they would both be free. Surely he had no desire to run the business.

"Fine. I'll see you there." She took Ella's hand and walked out of the office. Her heart filled with old resentments and new frustrations. There had to be a way around this ridiculous will. Why would her father do this to her? He knew how she and her mother hated the lodge. It was the reason her parents had divorced.

But Mack was right. She couldn't allow the estate to go to auction. She needed the money she could get from selling. There was no hope of paying off Ella's hospital bills otherwise. Her father owed her that much. At least then the lodge would finally justify its existence.

Somehow she had to convince Mack that it was in everyone's best interest to cut their losses and sell. There were too many memories here, too much pain and sadness. Adding Mack into the mix was only making it worse and stirring up another collection of painful incidents.

There was nothing at all at Longleaf Lodge and Campgrounds that she wanted. Except out from under it and hopefully enough money to be free of debt.

Mack watched Carly stride stiff-backed through the office door, pulling her daughter along with her as if she couldn't get away fast enough. He'd hoped that coming back to Hastings after all this time would have softened her attitude. Given her response to the conditions of the will, she hadn't changed at all. Emotionally, that is. Physically, she was very different. The last time he'd seen her was when she was seventeen and she'd made her last visit to the lodge after her parents split. She'd been every inch a tomboy. That skinny kid was now an incredibly lovely woman, with soft curves and an inner strength that showed in her fawn-colored eyes.

Her warm brown hair was no longer pulled back into a sassy ponytail, but fell in soft sections around her pretty face, calling attention to her big brown eyes. Unfortunately, her old resentment toward her father—and to him— was still in evidence. Her parents' divorce had changed everything and he didn't fully understand why.

He'd hoped they could finally move beyond the tensions of the past and become friends again. He'd never understood why Carly ran so hot and cold toward him. They'd even shared a kiss on her last visit to the lodge. One that he still regretted, though he'd never been able to forget it. She'd been younger than him, and the boss's daughter. A combination nearly impossible to overcome. The same way his feelings for Carly had never been overcome. And after seeing her again today he knew he hadn't gotten over her. She still held a part of his heart.

A short while later, Mack pulled to a stop in front of the Longleaf Lodge. Lucy hopped out as soon as he turned off the engine. The parking spots were empty. Carly hadn't arrived yet. He wasn't sure she would. Her feelings toward her father ran deep, and he feared they were strong enough that she would stand by and let the lodge be put up for auction. The last thing he wanted to see.

He loved this place. It had been his second home since he was fourteen, and Wade Porter the father he'd never had. He stepped into the lodge, the sense of peace and welcome settling on his shoulders the way it always did.

Dwayne and Thelma Thompson looked up from behind the registration desk. The couple had worked for Carly's father as long as Mack could remember. Dwayne was general manager and Thelma kept the books and ran the lodge. They were as much a part of the lodge as Wade.

Dwayne came toward him. "How did it go?"

Mack shook his head. "Wade threw everyone a curveball." He filled them in, watching the surprise on the couple's faces. "Did you have any idea he was going to do this?"

Dwayne shook his head. "I knew he was trying to get Carly to come home. He hoped she'd change her mind and keep the lodge, but I had no idea about those conditions."

Thelma met his gaze. "Did you see Carly?"

"I did. She looks great." He couldn't hold back a smile. "Her little girl looks just like her."

"I wish her daddy could have seen her. Is she coming to stay here?"

"She doesn't have a choice. It's a condition of the will."

"Oh, then I'd better get the apartment ready."

After his wife left the room, Dwayne leaned closer. "Tell me the truth. Do you think Carly will go along with this arrangement? Do you think she'll keep the lodge?"

Mack hated to kill the hope he saw in the older man's eyes. "I wouldn't count on it. The first thing she asked the attorney was how soon she could put the place on the market. She wants no part of this place. If it wasn't for me being listed as an heir, she'd have a real estate agent out here pounding a for-sale sign into the ground."

Dwayne shook his head. "Maybe when she's been here a few days, she'll remember the good times. There were a lot of them before the divorce."

"I don't understand why she doesn't."

"That last year was hard on everyone. Wade and Sonia were at each other's throats every day, and Carly was caught in the middle. She probably felt she needed to stand by her mom, who was being mistreated."

"Wade never mistreated anyone."

"That was Sonia's side of the story. I always told Wade he should have fought for joint custody, but he thought Carly would be better off with her mom."

Lucy came in from the backyard. "Uncle Mack, is that little girl and her mom coming here to live? It would be nice to have a friend to play with."

"I'm not sure, kiddo. We'll have to wait and see."

Car doors slamming drew everyone's attention. The lodge door opened, and Carly and Ella entered, stopping inside the entrance. Carly slowly surveyed the large main room, and from the expression on her face, Mack's hopes began to deflate.

Having Carly in his life again was going to be more awkward than he'd expected. He had wondered if seeing her once more would have any effect on him, and it had. The old attraction was stirring to life again. She was still the most beautiful woman he'd ever seen, though much of the sparkle she used to exude was missing now. One thing he couldn't deny was that seeing her back in the lodge felt right.

"Welcome home."

She met his gaze, her brown eyes hard and determined. "My home is in Atlanta."

His last thread of hope vanished. He'd envisioned a new beginning for them, and a return to the old friendship they'd shared. Getting Carly to remember how happy she'd been at Longleaf Lodge might be a bigger task than he'd anticipated.

From the look on her face, she had no warm memories of the lodge, and if that was true then his hopes of keeping the place and providing a real home for his niece were slim. For the first time in sixty years, the Longleaf Lodge might not be in the Porter family.

And that broke his heart.

Carly was keenly aware of the intense stare Mack was sending in her direction, and she tried to ignore her fluttering pulse. His blue gaze had always had an unsettling effect on her, and she wasn't pleased to find that it still had the power to elevate her heart rate. Her gaze traveled around the large open room that was the heart of the lodge. The place hadn't changed at all. Three large leather sofas were positioned in front of the tall stone fireplace. A wagon wheel light fixture hung overhead. Floor-to-ceiling windows at the far end of the room looked out onto the beauty of Lake Hope with comfy furniture arranged to take in the view.

For a brief moment she remembered her days as a child when she had found so much joy and comfort within the large log lodge. But that was long ago, before her world had fractured.

Dwayne stepped forward, arms outstretched. "Welcome back, Cupcake."

Her heart warmed at the old nickname, because that was her favorite dessert, and his wife, Thelma, made the best ones. She accepted his hug willingly. The Thompsons were the only bright light in this trip back to Hastings.

"It's so good to see you again. Ella, this is Mr. Dwayne, a very old friend."

Ella smiled up at him. "Why do you call her Cupcake?"

Thelma hurried across the room from the direction of the west wing, where the owner's apartment was located. "Because she couldn't get enough cupcakes as a little girl." Thelma hugged her and placed her hands on Carly's cheeks, her eyes moist as she looked at her.

"It's so good to have you back. We've missed you." She transferred her attention to Ella. "And look at this sweet thing. You look just like your mama did when she was little."

"Can I have a nickname, too?"

"Of course. What's your favorite snack?"

"Cookies."

"Then that'll be your pet name. Cookie."

Ella nodded and smiled. "We're Cupcake and Cookie, that's cool."

Lucy entered the room and hurried toward the new arrivals. "Hi. I'm Lucy. You wanna come play with me on the swing set?"

Ella glanced up at her with a hopeful face. How could she refuse? Besides, she needed to run off some energy after the long drive to Mississippi.

"Go ahead, sweetie. But don't wander off. Stay close by."

The girls dashed toward the back door as Thelma slipped her arm in Carly's and led her toward the hall off the registration desk. "I have the apartment all ready for you and Ella. All your daddy's things have been packed up and stored for when you're ready to go through them."

Carly stopped in her tracks. There was no way she was going to stay in her father's home—the section of the lodge that had been designed for her family. Too many bad memories. "No. We'll just stay in one of the guest rooms. We won't be here that long." She slanted a glance at Mack, who had been standing at the desk silently, studying her with his piercing blue eyes filled with confusion and a bit of disgust, no doubt. Her only goal now was to convince Mack to sell the property as quickly as possible. Surely he had a life elsewhere?

Thelma exchanged looks with her husband. "Well, of course, dear. Right this way." Thelma led her to the other side of the lodge, settling her in the corner room with the best view. No memories here.

"Well, I'll let you get settled. You know where everything is, but if you need anything you let me know."

She gave the woman another hug. Dwayne and Thelma had been the two constants in her life. The dear aunt and uncle she'd never had. Her dad was always busy running the campgrounds and keeping the place in order. Her mom used to manage the lodge but stopped when things became strained between her and Carly's father. Dwayne and Thelma, however, had never changed.

"I was sorry to hear about your husband."

"Thank you. I miss him." No more than at

this moment. Troy always knew the right thing to do.

It took her only a few moments to unpack the few belongings she'd brought. If they were going to stay here for any length of time she'd have to go shopping soon. Her gaze drifted to the large window that looked out over the lake and the long sloping lawn. Age-old oaks, sweetgums and longleaf pines, for which the lodge took its name, swayed in the late-spring breeze. Farther along the back, tucked in a pine grove, was a small worship center.

A yard swing hanging from the branch of a massive live oak at the edge of the water was still there. Swings were a symbol of the lodge. Her dad had them everywhere. They were on each porch around the main lodge; each campground had a swing, and picnic tables and swings were scattered around the pool area. There was a private one on their apartment porch. But the one by the water had always been her favorite. Her dad said swings were the perfect place to think, reflect and relax.

And now two little girls were enjoying the swing set her father had built for her closer to the lodge. Lucy, with her curly blond hair and blue eyes, and Ella, her brown-eyed, brown-haired treasure. It was nice to see her daughter with a friend. She'd been without any for a long while.

Stepping into the hall, she glanced up to see Mack at the top of the stairs. She braced for a barrage of questions about her not staying in her dad's rooms. He wouldn't understand her feelings. He had always been her dad's ally.

"Your daughter is adorable."

His comment caught her off guard. "Thank you. She's my whole life."

"I understand that now more than ever."

"What do you mean?"

"I'm Lucy's guardian. She came to live with me six months ago. I've had a steep learning curve on fatherhood."

Mack, a dad? She hadn't expected that. She'd assumed he was watching his niece, not raising her, though she remembered he'd always been good with the kids who came to the lodge and campgrounds. "Where's Valerie?"

He took a long moment to respond, and she could tell by the shadows in his eyes something was wrong.

"She got into some trouble. She's in prison for the next decade."

Her heart clenched. "Oh, Mack." She reached out and touched his arm. "I'm so sorry to hear that." Valerie had always been troubled, even back when Carly first met Mack. She'd run away from home, and Mack and his mom had been sick with worry. His dad had walked out on the family when Mack was a toddler.

Mack laid his hand on top of hers, sending a strange current along her nerves, leaving her with a conflicted desire to pull away and remain at the same time.

"She tried to turn her life around, even got a good job on the coast and moved Mom down there to help with Lucy, but after Mom passed away, she fell back into her old ways. Thankfully, she arranged for me to have Lucy."

"So you live on the coast now?"

"Gulfport for the time being."

She pulled her hand from beneath his, rubbing it slightly to dispel the lingering sensation of his broad palm. "You're moving?" A wry smile moved his lips.

"I'd like to raise Lucy here at the lodge. She needs a family, and between me and the Thompsons she could have a good life."

A long-forgotten memory flashed into her mind of a childhood spent outdoors, hiking, canoeing, climbing trees and sitting around campfires. It was quickly overshadowed by other memories of shouting and anger and betrayal. She squared her shoulders. "If you're trying to play on my sympathies, it won't work." She stepped past him and started down the stairs.

"I'm only telling you what I want for my niece. She deserves a real home, and I can only give her an apartment and part-time father."

Carly stopped. She was in a similar position, raising her daughter alone without a father. She understood his concerns. Looking over her shoulder, she met his gaze. "Lucy is very fortunate to have you, Mack."

"I'm the fortunate one. She's changed my life."

A thread of empathy fluttered along her nerves. "Children can do that." Her mind bloomed with a bouquet of sweet memories from childhood until the last one scrolled by, shading all the others in a dark cloud. She moved away toward the stairs.

"Carly, I was sorry to hear about your husband."

She spun around. "How did you know about that?"

"Your dad told me."

"How did he know? I never told him."

A deep frown creased Mack's forehead. "Why wouldn't you tell your father that your husband died?"

"A better question might be why would he care?"

"What? Carly, how can you—"

She hurried down the stairs and made her

way quickly to the backyard. The fragrant spring air filled her lungs with the familiar scent of water and earth and pine. Giggles floating on the air from the swing set made her smile. It was so good to hear her daughter laugh again. She knew how hard and unfeeling her words sounded to others, but they didn't understand. Her father was the one who'd destroyed everything. She swallowed the old hurt, and smiled at Ella and Lucy on the swing.

"Hello, girls. Are you having fun?"

Ella grinned and dragged her toes on the ground to slow the swing. "This is the best swing ever. It goes really high."

"Mr. Wade built it a long time ago." Lucy made the announcement with a very serious tone.

"I know. He built it for me when I was your age."

"Who's Mr. Wade?"

Ella's question nearly brought Carly to her knees. In her animosity toward her father, she had totally forgotten that he was Ella's grandpa, too. "Mr. Wade was my daddy." She had some explaining to do. Coming back here was going to be much harder than she'd ever dreamed. "Ella, why don't you come inside for a moment and I'll show you which room we're in. Then you can come back out and play with Lucy."

"Okay."

Lucy followed them inside.

"Mommy, can we stay here for a long time? I like it."

Even her own daughter was falling under the spell of the lodge. Carly's heart wrenched. "We'll see, honey. I don't know yet how long we'll be here."

"I hope it's a whole week because I want to play more with Lucy."

She'd never felt so outnumbered. Everyone but her wanted her to stay at Longleaf. Why couldn't they understand that the memories were too painful, the betrayal too deep.

This place had torn her family apart.

She could never live here again.

Chapter Two

Mack had been patient long enough. He'd held his tongue during the delicious feast Thelma had prepared. As they sat around one of the large tables in the lodge dining room, Dwayne and Thelma tried their best to keep the conversation light by talking about amusing guests that had stayed at the lodge and reminiscing about happy times in the past. Carly had only nodded and made a few muffled responses, choosing to stare at her food most of the time. The girls had helped keep the meal from being awkward by sharing the fun they'd had during the day.

When Carly announced that she was putting Ella to bed, Mack had to speak up. Time was crucial, and he wasn't about to let Longleaf Lodge go to auction and end up with an owner who didn't understand or appreciate the history and significance of the place. He stopped her at the foot of the stairs.

"We need to talk, Carly. We can't put this off any longer." The look on her face told him that was exactly what she wanted to do. She glanced up at her daughter, who was hurrying up to her room, and her expression shifted to one of resignation. When she faced him again, her brown eyes were filled with determination.

"Fine. I'll come back down after I put Ella to bed."

Mack watched her as she took the steps, each graceful movement reminding him of his old attraction. His heart skipped a beat and he turned away. That was a long time ago and the will loomed between them now, making any kind of friendship difficult.

He stood by the stone fireplace staring into the empty firebox, his mind scrolling through old memories, all of them centering around Carly. He'd fallen for her the first time he'd seen her—not in a romantic way since she'd only been twelve, but she was cute and smart and her cheery personality had been adorable. As the years went on, she'd changed into a feisty teenager with a heart for the guests. When she'd turned sixteen, things had started to shift. Mack had admired her from afar. Her being the boss's daughter and an underage teen were obstacles that prevented any action on his part. Time had always been their enemy. A perpetual wrong-place wrong-time scenario.

He turned when he sensed a presence behind him. Carly came slowly toward him as if fearful of getting too close. He couldn't help but wonder why. "Is Ella okay?"

"All settled in. What about Lucy?"

"She's watching a movie. I'll check on her in a minute."

She nodded, resting a hand on the mantel and glancing up at the top of the stone chimney. "I never understood why you'd put a fireplace in a Mississippi house. We rarely used this in the winter."

"True, our weather stays pretty warm in the southern part of the state, but I think people like them not for the warmth of the fire, but for the ambience. A fireplace is comforting. It makes us feel safe, as if we're protected from the forces beyond the flames."

"That's very poetic."

He had to chuckle at that. "Yeah. I don't know where that came from. I seem to have all kinds of new viewpoints since I became Lucy's guardian." He could see the questions forming in Carly's eyes, and he didn't want to be distracted by talking about his niece. They had more important things to sort out.

He motioned to the leather chairs at the side of the fireplace.

Carly didn't wait for him to start. She sat on the edge of the cushion, stiff-backed and serious. "I spoke with a real estate agent today and he gave me a rough estimate of the value of the land and the lodge. I think the simplest solution would be for you to buy me out. Then you can have Longleaf, and I can take my share of profits and go home."

"Profits? Is that all the lodge means to you? Money?"

She swiped her hair behind her ear. "Yes."

He knew that gesture. It meant she was hiding what she was really feeling. It didn't make any sense. Unless he was misreading her. It had been a long time since they'd seen each other. Old hurts resurfaced without warning. "I never realized how much like your mother you were."

"What's that supposed to mean?"

"Nothing. Sorry. I was out of line." He knew she wasn't like her mother. "Carly, I can't buy you out. I know what this place is worth, and there's no way I can raise that kind of money."

"That's what loans are for."

"I'm a cop, a sergeant with the sheriff's department. I've been flipping houses on the side to make ends meet. Why don't you buy me out? Then you can sell and have all the money you need for your big-city lifestyle."

"I'm an administrative assistant for a friend's clothing-design business. Not exactly a cash cow."

"Then that leaves us with only one option. We have to follow the dictates of the will."

Carly leaned back in the chair, her shoulders slumped. "I can't stay here for two months. I have a life in Atlanta. Besides, what makes you think we can get the lodge open and running again?"

"I already spoke to Dwayne. He says the staff he let go when Wade got sick are all anxious to come back to work. He thinks we can reopen in a week, maybe two. With you and I taking up some of the slack, we can start hosting guests soon after that. He gets calls every day asking when they will reopen."

Carly tapped her thumbnail against her teeth. "It sounds impossible."

"I won't lie to you, it's not going to be easy. A large hotel chain built a resort-type facility across the lake, which has lured a lot of guests away. Wade was very discouraged."

"Then what makes you think we can make a go of this place in only two months? What's the point if we're only going to sell out at the end?"

"I think there are still a lot of tourists who want a peaceful, calm outdoor experience. The hotel is pricey, their food is pricey and there's always something going on. Longleaf offers a slower pace, an escape from that kind of environment. It appeals to an entirely different demographic."

"I'm not convinced." She crossed her arms. "Why do you want to keep the lodge?"

"I loved it here. I loved your dad. I'd like Lucy to grow up with this kind of home, free to run and play outdoors, and surrounded by a sense of permanence. This has been in your family since your grandfather built the lodge in the seventies. It has a history. Your dad loved this place."

Carly's mouth pinched into a tight line. "I know. He loved it more than anything or anyone."

"What does that mean?"

She brushed off his comment.

Mack's chest tightened. He was beginning to think Carly would never agree to any plan he suggested. She wanted no part of the lodge and he didn't understand why unless, like her mother, she was more interested in a luxurious life in Atlanta. He found that hard to accept. He remembered how much Carly had loved the lodge growing up. There had to be a way to convince Carly to at least make an attempt to save the lodge. It's what Wade had wanted. Maybe he could offer a compromise. It wasn't exactly honest, but he had to do something to break this logjam they were facing. If he had to fudge a little, then so be it.

He sent up a prayer that Carly would agree to his next suggestion. "What if we work together to get the place up and running? We clean up the grounds and maybe update the interior of the lodge to make it more appealing. Then we would have a better chance of getting top dollar."

"You would agree to that?"

"It's not what I want, but I don't want to stand by and let the place be auctioned off. It would break your father's heart. We don't have time to mull this over. We have to make a decision now. If we do nothing, then we both lose. Is that really what you want?"

The shadow of doubt in her eyes gave Mack a ray of hope. Maybe deep down she really did care. He just had to find a way to make her remember.

"I think I can do that. As long as we agree our goal is to make the lodge attractive to prospective buyers, and as long as you understand that I don't want Longleaf."

Mack shoved aside his twinge of guilt for misleading her. "I understand."

"Good." Carly stood, meeting his gaze and sending a strange longing through him. Seeing her here the way he'd always remembered was a bittersweet moment, and he wanted it to last.

"We should get started in the morning right after breakfast. We need to get an overview of the estate, see the condition of the grounds so we can prioritize the needs."

Carly looked reluctant. "So soon?"

"We can't waste any more time. I thought you were anxious to get back home."

"Fine. I'll see you in the morning." She walked off and up the stairs, never looking back.

Mack watched her go, his heart sinking slowly. Dwayne strolled to his side, watching as Carly disappeared.

"How did it go?"

"I had to compromise on the truth a little."

"How so?"

"I got her to agree to stay and fix the place with the intention of attracting a good buyer."

"Did you both agree that you want to sell?"

"No. But I'm hoping that after she's been here awhile she'll remember how much she loved the place and she won't want to let it go."

"I wouldn't hold your breath. From what I've

seen so far, whatever chased her away from Longleaf hasn't softened with time."

"What was it, do you know?"

"Not really, but it had something to do with her mother, I can tell you that."

Mack went upstairs to tuck Lucy in, mulling over Dwayne's comment about Carly's mom. He had no idea what had gone wrong, but it had changed everything in the blink of an eye. Wade had never been the same after his wife had left him. Carly had only returned once after that, a year later and left suddenly after they'd shared that one unbelievable kiss. He'd forgotten for a moment that she was the boss's daughter. But he just couldn't ignore how the moment had seemed so right, and the kiss, as brief as it had been, had shifted his world. So much so that he'd made a date with Natalie Reynolds, his old girlfriend just to forget the whole incident. He'd taken her to the lodge for a canoe ride. Carly had left the next day, leaving him confused and guilt ridden, and with pain he'd never experienced before. The memory could still send tiny pinpricks of hurt along his nerves.

As much as he hated to admit it, Carly was part of his life and always would be. No matter how much he wished he could stop caring. It would be easier to stop breathing.

* * *

Carly watched her sleeping daughter. She envied the ability to simply set aside the events of the day and drift off. Her thoughts were too stirred up to consider sleeping. She needed to move, to do something. Slipping from the room, she made her way quietly downstairs, relieved to find the lodge silent and empty.

Carly fingered the key in her hand, fighting the knots in her stomach. She wasn't sure why she was doing this. She didn't want to remember the past, but something inside her compelled her to visit the place where she'd grown up.

Inserting the key, she turned the lock and opened the door, stepping into the rooms that had been her childhood home. The west side of the lodge consisted of a two-bedroom apartment, so large and spacious it had never felt like an apartment. With open rooms, a second floor and wide private deck, it had provided a sanctuary for the family away from the constant flow of guests staying at the lodge.

Carly stepped into the rooms, bracing for a barrage of bad memories. What slammed into her, however, were the good ones from when she was small. The winter evenings spent in front of the fire, the Christmas tree sitting by the large windows looking out onto the lake.

She turned when she heard tapping on the doorframe. Dwayne stepped in, a small smile on his lined face.

"It's good to see you in these rooms again, Carly. They've missed you."

She set her jar. "I doubt that." She noticed a collection of photographs on the mantel. She picked up one, shocked to see a picture of Ella when she was small. "What are these doing here? How did he get this?"

Dwayne tugged on his ear and grinned. "Your husband sent them. He felt it was the right thing to do. Wade wanted to see his grandchild."

A hot flush washed through her. Of course her father would want to see Ella. Troy tried repeatedly to convince her to visit her father and bring Ella, but her anger and hurt had run too deep. She never wanted to feel that sense of betrayal again. Yet Troy had betrayed her, too, and gone behind her back.

"Your papa cherished those. It wasn't all bad, you know. You were happy here. But after your mom came back and took you away, nothing was the same. Especially your father."

"What do you mean, came back?"

"Don't you remember? It was that summer you were sixteen. Your mom walked out real sudden-like. She was gone a week, then she showed back up, caused a scene and took you away. Your dad never told me what happened, but it nearly killed him. It took him years to fight through that."

Carly shook her head. "No. That can't be true. He caused her to leave. It was all his fault."

Dwayne studied her a moment. "Maybe things aren't quite the way you remember them. When we're young, events don't always make sense."

She crossed her arms over her chest and set her jaw. "No. It made sense." She knew exactly why her mother had left.

"Well, I'll leave you be."

Carly rubbed her forehead, struggling to understand what Dwayne had said. What had he meant about her mother leaving? She tried to remember but came up empty. Climbing the stairs, she went into her old room. It looked different yet still the same. A new solid blue bedspread replaced her flowered one, and most of her posters and decorations were gone. Apparently her dad hadn't done the old make-my-child's-room-a-shrine thing, which only proved that he hadn't really cared for her the way she'd believed.

Her old desk was still there, and she sat down and scanned the items on top. Her old digital camera. It was the last gift her father had given her, and she'd carried it everywhere. She'd loved to capture those once-in-a-lifetime moments where the sun shone just right over the lake or the moon glistened through the pines leaving rays of white light on the trail. She'd decided she would become a professional photographer. Sadly, she'd lost sight of that dream along the way.

Sliding open the middle drawer where she kept all her special mementoes, she touched the assortment, little flashes of memories flaring, each one bringing a warmth to her chest. Her fingers picked up a small silver earring inlaid with a pearl and a diamond. A lance of pain and sadness sliced her heart in two. It wasn't her mother's. She had pierced ears. This was a clip-on and she'd found it on the floor of her dad's car. Proof of what her mother had told her. The reason her family had been torn apart.

Her dad's unfaithfulness.

She shoved the jewelry back in the drawer, slammed it shut. Tears welled up in her eyes as she hurried back to the main room of the lodge. She wanted to go home. She wanted out of this horrible arrangement, and she wanted away from all the memories.

Just then, her phone rang. She recognized the name of the company calling, and her throat closed as it always did when the bill collectors harassed her. They had no problem calling at all hours. There was no point in answering because there was nothing she could tell them. She still didn't have the money to pay them. She shoved the phone back into her pocket, unwilling to even contemplate the consequences she might be facing soon. She prayed that a buyer could be found for the lodge quickly; otherwise, she and Ella might be homeless.

Carly took as much time at breakfast as she could, hoping to postpone the tour of Longleaf Lodge with Mack. Despite her issues with him, he still had a way of stirring up feelings she didn't want stirred. Her relationship with him had always been conflicted. She'd been drawn to him since the moment they'd met, but his close relationship with her dad had always filled her with resentment. She envied the closeness they had shared and the time they'd spent together. So many years away from the lodge and Mack hadn't changed anything. It was a realization she had no idea how to process.

Carly pushed back from the table in the large kitchen. "Thank you for the breakfast, Thelma. It was wonderful as usual."

"I'm loving cooking for you again, Cupcake."

"Are you sure you don't mind watching Ella while we're gone?"

"No indeed. I plan on making special pancakes for the girls when they get up, and Dwayne is bringing the dogs over from our place. They'll enjoy playing with them."

"Dogs? Is Bully still around?" Her dad's black Lab had been as much a part of the family as she was.

"No. Bully went on to his reward. Your dad got a German shepherd from a friend and called him Riley. He's a good watchdog. Then Dwayne and I rescued two little Lhasa–shih tzu mix pups. Poppy and Petunia. Sweet little things. They like to cuddle."

"Ella will love them. She's always wanted a dog. Thanks again, Thelma. I don't think we'll be long."

Thelma patted her arm. "Cupcake, try and keep an open mind, okay? Make sure you see everything the way it is, not the way you remember."

Carly wasn't sure what Thelma was trying to convey but she promised. Thelma was a wise woman, and it wouldn't hurt to take her words to heart.

Mack was standing by the golf cart wearing that crooked grin of his when she stepped onto the wide front porch.

"Good morning, Carly. Are you ready?"

"As I'll ever be." She tried to halt the wave of appreciation that spiraled up unexpectedly into her chest. Mack had always been too handsome for his own good. A large part of his appeal was that he had no idea what his boy-next-door good looks and athletic build did to women. She recalled, as a teen, many of her girlfriends sighing loudly when he smiled in their direction.

Mack set the cart in motion as soon as she was seated. She pulled her old camera from her pocket and held it in her lap.

"Whatcha got there?"

"My old camera I found when I was in the apartment."

Mack shot a glance in her direction. "You were in the apartment?"

Carly didn't want to talk about that. "Where are we going to start?"

"I thought we'd go by the pool area first."

Carly tried to keep her eyes forward and avoid the stunning beauty of her father's legacy. If she started to look beyond her resentment, who knew what she might find. It was one reason she'd picked up the camera. It was easier to view things through a lens than experience it outright. A camera allowed you to see without getting emotionally involved.

Mack steered the cart through the pine trees and made a left turn, bringing them to the pool house and snack bar at one end of the large rectangular swimming pool. He pulled to a stop and glanced around.

"It looks like it's in good shape." A large cover was stretched over the water to protect it from debris and accidents.

"It is. Wade upgraded it a couple years ago—added the pool cover and renovated the kitchen in the snack bar. Of course we'll need to clean the place and treat the pool water."

"So we can have this up and running quickly?"

"Sure. It's warm enough."

"It's early May. The pool should have been open already."

"It would be if the lodge were open."

"Right." Even with all that had happened during the last two days, Carly found it hard to remember that the lodge was closed. Her dad never closed. For any reason. It was one of the things her mother had hated. She'd wanted to take vacations to other places, to go on a cruise, but her father had refused to leave the lodge for any length of time. She pointed her small camera and took a few pictures.

"Trying to recapture memories?"

Carly shook her head, avoiding his gaze. "I want to post pictures online to show prospective buyers all the amenities. The pictures need to evoke an emotion."

"Do they evoke emotions in you?"

She ignored his question. "Where to next?"

Mack headed out toward the perimeter of the land. As far as she knew there was nothing there but piney woods, but in a few minutes Mack turned into a camping area with five large concrete parking pads. "What's this?"

"Wade added RV sites. They were very successful. He was hoping to add more."

When she'd lived here, the only camping facilities were for tents and small campers. They made a swing through that section, then Mack drove toward the lake and stopped near a grove of live oaks near the bank. He stopped the cart and stared out onto the water.

Carly waited for him to speak, but he seemed lost in thought. "Why did we stop?"

"This is where we said goodbye to your dad."

"What do you mean?"

"We scattered his ashes right out there on the lake that he loved."

Carly's throat closed up. Tears stung the backs of her eyes in a swirl of mixed emotions. "The *only* thing he loved." Mack looked at her, a deep frown on his face.

"That's not true. He loved you."

She didn't want to argue with him, so she changed the subject. "We should keep going. We've only seen a small part of the grounds. I need to get back to Ella."

"Ella and Lucy are just fine." Mack started the cart with more acceleration than necessary, forcing them both back against the seat. He sped through the trees, slowing when they reached the two hiking trails. They began at a central point, each with a sign bearing the name of the trail, the length, and a small map etched into the thick wooden sign. The Piney Woods Trail, and the Rocky Creek Trail. But there was a third sign now. The Carly's Hill Trail. "I don't understand. When did he add this trail?"

"Shortly after you left one summer you returned." He steered the cart down the narrow trail. The ground slowly rose with each turn until they perched on a rise overlooking the water. She recognized it as her favorite spot to think or read or just look at the lake. Her thoughts were full of old memories, and she tried desperately to understand what she was seeing. Mack's soft voice intruded into her thoughts.

"The old fallen tree had rotted away, so that's why he built the bench."

Her gaze searched the area. She hadn't even noticed the bench. A nice sturdy one with a slatted back and curved arms, and a slice of tree trunk on the side situated perfectly as a side table. She'd always complained that she had to sit her bottle of water on the ground.

Carly struggled to find words. It didn't make any sense. Why would he construct a trail just for her?

"Why didn't you come to the funeral?" Mack asked.

Her defenses kicked in. "It wasn't a funeral. Only a memorial service."

"You should have been here."

"And my dad should have—" She snapped her lips shut. "We should see the rest of the property."

Mack stiffened but kept silent, and he drove back down the trail and headed toward the five cabins. "The cabins need work. Two of them are in good condition, but the other three need electrical and plumbing work, and one of them is in need of major repairs."

He drove past the row of cabins situated near the lake edge.

"Stop," she said. Mack brought the cart to a halt. "Why is this cabin boarded up?"

Mack inhaled a slow breath before answering. "It's not usable right now."

"Why not?"

He leaned his forearms on the steering wheel. "The cabin was rented to a group of college students who got drunk and trashed the place. They left holes in the wall, pulled the plumbing from the bathroom, destroyed kitchen appliances and broke the windows. Everything inside needs to be replaced."

Carly's hopes sank. "We've never had anything like this happen before. Our guests were always respectful of the property. Did Dad report this to the police?"

"He did, and they were fined and ordered to pay for the damage. They were supposed to work on it themselves, but your dad got sick so the money came in handy, but the repairs are now on us."

"Is there any way we can get this cabin ready to rent?"

"No."

Carly's hopes took another nosedive. How many other areas would have to be left untouched in order to get the lodge open by the deadline? She looked away from the damaged cabin, frowning at the empty landscape ahead. "Where's the canoe livery? It was always right near the cabins."

"It's moved farther down the bank. It's its own destination now."

Mack drove down a new gravel path she didn't remember. Pulling into a small parking area with a neatly laid out path leading to the triangle-shaped canoe stand. But instead of the usual eight, there were only two, and beside it was another stand that held four colorful kayaks. Beyond that, resting on the grassy bank, were three johnboats.

"Where are the canoes?"

"Several of them are in need of repairs. Wade never got around to fixing them. The kayaks are a new addition. The younger guests prefer them to the canoes."

Carly tapped in canoe repair to her phone list of things needing to be done before they could reopen. Mack turned the cart around and headed back to the lodge. "The Piney Woods Trail needs clearing. They had a high-wind storm a month or so ago and the path is littered with limbs and debris. That was right after Wade got sick and closed the lodge, so it never got taken care of."

Carly added that to her list. The number of areas needing attention was long and time-consuming, and they hadn't even made a survey of the main lodge and what might need doing there. "I don't know how we can open in a week."

"Then we'll open in two."

"No. I want this place on the market as soon as possible."

"Why are you in such a hurry to unload the lodge? This is your heritage."

"I don't live here. I live in Atlanta, and I have no desire to run the campgrounds. So there's no reason to hang around and waste time. The sooner we sell the better."

"So it's all about the money with you?"

"Not in the way you mean."

"What other way is there?"

"I need to get back." She was not about to discuss the sad state of her financial affairs with him.

The muscle in his jaw flexed as he accelerated. They were halfway to the lodge before he spoke again.

"How did your husband die? Wade never told me."

Reliving that moment never got any easier. "Heart attack. We were having a cookout with friends and he went inside to get more burgers and never came out. A friend went in to check on him and found him."

Mack reached over and took her hand. "I'm

sorry, Carly. I shouldn't have asked. It must have been hard for you and Ella."

"She was only three at the time, so she only has faint memories of him. I keep a picture in her room so she won't forget what he looked like." He'd been a wonderful father and husband. The perfect mate.

Thankfully they had arrived at the lodge. Carly got out and strode toward the lodge. Mack called her name, but she waved him off. "I'm going to check with Thelma. She has a list of things needing to be done in the lodge. We'll get together later and prioritize."

She could feel his gaze burning into her back. But she refused to get caught up in pointless sentiment and old memories. The goal was to get the lodge ready for the market. She was already thinking of how to photograph the areas to best advantage and upgrade the website to be more user-friendly.

The sooner she could attract a buyer, the sooner they could all go back to the way things were.

Chapter Three

Dwayne was waiting in the golf cart shed when Mack pulled up. He came over and rested a hand on the cart's roof. "Well, how did it go?"

Mack leaned back, resting his hands on his thighs. "I'm not sure."

Dwayne chuckled. "That's a nice clear answer."

"I showed her everything, even the new trail Wade laid out for her. I guess I was expecting some sort of emotional reaction, but she was cool and detached the whole time."

"That doesn't sound like the girl I remember."

Mack nodded in agreement. "I think she was surprised by the changes, but I can't tell if she approved or not. She took some pictures."

"Really? Why?"

"She said to use them on the website and in the real estate listings."

"She's that anxious to unload the place?"

Mack rubbed his forehead. "It's like she can't stand to even be at the lodge."

"I'm not surprised. Her mama did a number on her. You know she refused to stay in Wade's apartment."

"Yeah. I noticed. How can she be so blind to what a wonderful man her father was?"

Dwayne adjusted his cap. "Maybe because someone else was standing between her and the truth."

"Her mother. I get it. I don't know what happened, but I remember the arguments. They were loud and hurtful."

Dwayne shook his head. "That wasn't the only thing going on, you know."

"What else could there have been?"

The older man patted his shoulder. "You'll have to work that out with Carly. And if I were you I'd let her know what you actually want out of this arrangement, because when she finds out you weren't serious about selling and were only agreeing to buy time, she'll explode. Carly has many of Wade's good qualities, but she got some bad ones from her mother—an explosive temper and the ability to carry a grudge. Especially when it involves someone she cares about."

Mack made his way back to the lodge trying to decipher the things Dwayne had said. He'd had the feeling his friend was trying to tell him something important without actually saying it, which was very uncharacteristic of him. He was usually a straight-talking kind of guy.

Whatever had happened between Wade and his wife had been enough to turn Carly against her dad. Which made no sense because she'd always worshipped him, following him around, helping with all the work around the lodge. Her pride in the lodge had been inspiring.

Mack walked up the steps to the front porch, Riley trotting happily beside him as his escort. A glance at his watch reminded him that it was nearly time for a call from his sister. Inside the lodge he looked for Lucy. Thelma glanced up from the registration desk and smiled.

"Lucy and Ella are on the swings out back. I think that's their new favorite spot."

The girls had hit it off and Mack was grateful. The last six months had been hard on his niece, losing her grandma, her mom, coming to live with him, then moving to Hastings and meeting more strangers. He wasn't sure how beneficial a call from Val would be, but it was the only thing his sister insisted on.

Mack stopped at the deck railing and watched the girls pushing the swing to the limits as they sang a song. He had no idea what it was, but Lucy had sung it often. Before he could call to his niece, Carly stepped onto the deck. The sunlight brought out the highlights in her brown hair.

She smiled as she watched the girls. "Ella has really bonded with your niece. I'm glad she has a friend here. Longleaf is very different from what she's used to."

"She seems to be adapting okay."

"I'm surprised. She's usually so shy, but things are different now."

"Things?"

Carly broke eye contact and called out to her daughter. Ella pouted. She was a cute kid.

"Lucy—" he held up his phone "—it's about time."

Lucy jumped off the swing and ran toward him. "We'll play later, Ella."

She hugged her uncle, and he turned and steered her into the house and found a quiet corner to wait for the phone call. Lucy held the cell like a lifeline, never taking her eyes from the screen.

Mack settled onto the couch, trying to quell

the rising tension in his chest. These moments were always so difficult. Lucy would become excited to talk to her mom, only to fall into deep sadness when it was over, and he was left to comfort her. He always felt like a failure and out of his depth on how to help.

His ringtone sounded, and Lucy punched the button before it finished. She sank onto the floor and spoke softly into the phone, her face aglow. He'd always loved his niece, and being her guardian had increased that tenfold. He had embraced the feeling and the responsibility. Now he would be lost without her. She meant everything to him, and he wanted to give her the world and protect her from any unhappiness. More than anything he wanted her to have a home.

When the phone call was over, Lucy sat with the phone in her lap, her eyes glassy with tears and her lips quivering. He braced himself for what was to come. Without a word he opened his arms and said her name. She jumped up and threw herself into his lap. He held her close as she cried.

"I want Mommy to come home."

"I know, sweetie, I know." He kissed her head and prayed for peace for her little broken heart.

As if sensing the child's mood, Petunia

came to the couch and jumped up, thrusting her furry head under Lucy's arm. The warm puppy momentarily stopped the tears.

Ella strolled into the room, then hurried out calling for her mom. Mack didn't have time to deal with Carly right now. Lucy was crying again. One hand gripped his shirt and the other hugged the little dog.

By the time Carly did enter the room, Lucy was regaining her composure. She had downgraded to sniffles, and her death grip on his shirt had eased.

Carly met his gaze, her expression asking if there was anything she could do. He made a slight movement of his head.

Ella broke away from her mom and came toward them. She stopped in front of his niece. "Lucy. Do you want to go swing? It always makes me happy after I've been sad."

To his surprise, Lucy nodded and sat up. Petunia jumped down and stood by Ella. Lucy took Ella's hand and the two walked slowly toward the back door, leaving Mack with a profound tenderness in his heart. *Thank You, Lord, for sending this little girl to be a friend to Lucy.*

Carly took a seat beside him, and he sensed she was bursting with questions. He sighed and rubbed the bridge of his nose. "Val calls

Lucy once a week. Lucy lives for those moments, but when they're over, she's crushed. I sometimes wish Val wouldn't call."

"Does Lucy ever visit her?"

"No. We both felt it wasn't good for her to see her mom that way."

"She's blessed to have you. You were always good with kids. I remember that one summer when that big family stayed here, the one with the seven kids. You came up with all kinds of fun activities for them."

Mack's pulse skipped a beat at the affectionate expression on her face. That was the Carly he remembered. Happy, optimistic and always full of energy. Maybe she did remember the good times at the lodge. "That was a fun time. I think the family stayed an extra week."

"They did, and I think they wanted to adopt you." She giggled at the memory.

Mack couldn't look away. At this moment, with her fawn-colored eyes lit with happiness and her sunny smile on display, that old dream he'd cherished about having Carly in his life was stirring again.

"I remember, but I already had a family right here with you and your dad."

Like the flip of the switch, Carly's good mood vanished. Her eyes darkened and the smile disappeared into a tight line. She stood.

"We need to get together with the Thompsons and determine how quickly we can get these repairs done. If we're going to have any hope of selling the lodge, we need to get it on the market ASAP."

"What's going on, Carly? What did I say?"

"Nothing. I told you. I don't want this place or...anyone connected with it."

Mack thought he saw a hint of tears in her eyes as she walked off, which made no sense. He ran a hand down the back of his neck, wondering if Lucy would be as hard a female to understand as Carly was.

Dwayne walked toward him and nodded to Carly as she hurried past him. He stared at Mack with a raised brow. "You have the look of a man with a dilemma."

"That's an understatement. I don't even have a clue what the problem is so I can start fixing it."

"You never did, kiddo."

"What does that mean?"

Dwayne shrugged and grinned. "Wade left his life's work to you *and* Carly. Think about it."

Mack shook his head. He was in no mood to unravel riddles. Granted, Wade's will was odd, to say the least, but Mack had always known his mentor would leave him something.

Wade knew how much Mack loved the lodge, but he'd expected a sum of money or maybe a piece of the land to call his own. Dwayne's comment suddenly loomed in his mind.

Why *had* Wade left the land to him and the lodge to his daughter? What was he hoping to accomplish? Mack had assumed it was his way of trying to remind Carly of her childhood here, the same way Mack was hoping to rekindle her love for Longleaf.

Could there be another reason? Nothing came to mind at the moment. Shoving the notion aside, he went in search of his niece to see if she'd recovered from the call from her mom. He found the two little girls on the yard swing under the giant live oak at the edge of the water. They had a book between them, oblivious to the world. He had a feeling Ella would be able to help Lucy more than he ever could.

It always helped to have a close friend who understood. Carly had been that friend for him after coming to work at the lodge. They'd enjoyed working together on the grounds and helping the guests in season.

All that mattered now was saving the estate. He had to get the Thompsons on board, and, God willing, the three of them could find a way to persuade Carly not to give up on the lodge.

Monday morning, Carly made an early escape from the lodge and headed out in her car. She needed to find some breathing space from all the memories and the pressure. Sunday had been filled with church and a nice dinner afterward. She'd managed to avoid everyone by taking Ella into Hastings for some mother-daughter mall shopping, then hiding in her room citing a need to catch up on work back home.

After putting on her blinker, she turned into the large parking lot of the Lake Hope Marina and parked her sedan. Situated five miles outside of Hastings, Lake Hope had become a thriving resort area. Along with the Longleaf Lodge and Campgrounds, there were rental cottages and fishing boats for hire. The Marina Village stores supplied not only the visitors but the local residents who lived and worked at the lake. Thelma had warned her the place had been completely redesigned and she hadn't been joking. The rustic low-roofed building of old had been replaced with a charming multi-building complex designed to resemble a small fishing village. Where the former structure had looked unsightly and unwelcoming, the new store invited everyone inside to explore and linger.

Carly started toward the main building, now

named the Lake Hope Marina Store. She and Ella had been in Hastings four days now and if they were staying the two months required by the will she needed to do some shopping. She was hoping she could cut that time in half and get back to her life in Atlanta, though.

Mack had organized a meeting with the Thompsons last night, and they had started to lay out a plan for reopening the lodge. Dwayne and Mack would work on the outside, getting the livery up and running, and clearing the trails, while she and Thelma concentrated on preparing the lodge for guests. Carly was hoping to freshen up the decor, provided there was enough funds in the account her father had left. Thelma had already started contacting former employees and offering them their jobs back and calling vendors to get the kitchen restocked and operating.

A father and young daughter passed by as Carly neared the entrance of the store, reminding her of the moment yesterday when she had stepped into the main room of the lodge and seen Lucy sobbing in Mack's lap. Ella had come to her, upset that her friend was crying. Her heart had ached for the child, but what had touched her most was Mack's tenderness with the little girl. He obviously cared deeply for his niece. It was one of the things she'd always loved and admired about him. He had a huge heart for others and a gentleness that reminded her of her dad.

Maybe that was why Mack and her dad had become so close—because they were so much alike and held the same interests. Qualities she must have lacked. Why else would her father prefer Mack to her?

The store was brightly lit, and a quick glance around made it easy to find the different departments. A two-lane checkout positioned near the door made purchasing items simple, quick and easy.

Carly took a few minutes to wander the aisles before tackling her shopping list. Dry goods were on one side, food and fishing supplies on the other. Bait and tackle, formerly housed inside the marina store, were now sold in a separate little shop.

"Carly? Carly Porter? Is that you?"

She spun around and saw a somewhat familiar face. It took her a second to recognize her old school friend Ashley Jenkins. They both squealed in excitement and hugged each other. "I can't believe you're still here."

"I can't believe you're back home."

"Oh, it's only temporary. I'll be leaving as soon as I can sell my dad's place."

"I know. I heard about the quirky will he left. Weird, huh?"

Carly had forgotten how small towns operated, and while Lake Hope wasn't exactly a town, it was a community, and news spread quickly among the residents. "I guess everyone knows then, huh?"

"Yep. How was it seeing Mack again? Any of the old sparks still there?"

"No. No sparks. There never was."

"You're kidding, right? There were plenty of sparks. Especially that last summer you were here." Ashley fanned her hand in front of her face. "If you hadn't run away, I was sure you two would have ended up engaged or something."

"I didn't run away. I had to leave suddenly."

Ashley stared at her a deep frown creasing her forehead. "I've never known you to hide from the truth, Carly. What happened that summer? You definitely ran away. You didn't even say goodbye to me."

Carly's stomach was churning and she wasn't sure why. "I'm sorry. It was a difficult time."

"Apparently." Ashley smiled and squeezed her hand. "I'm sorry. I didn't mean to stir up the past. I was sorry to hear about your husband. I know what you're going through. My husband died around the same time. A boating accident. It's been hard."

"Oh, Ash, I didn't know."

Ashley waved off her concern. "You've been gone. But I'm doing all right. I belong to a widow's therapy group. It's actually more like a support group. It's run by a psychologist, Nina Sinclair. She's wonderful. The women are all like you and me."

"I've already been through grief counseling."

"This is different. This is for widows who are further along on their journey and struggling with life alone, or coping with children, and sometimes learning to let go and love again. Mainly it's a place to go where we have others who really understand our situation. Here." Ashley scribbled on a piece of paper and handed it to her. "I'll tell Nina about you and if you feel you'd like to come, then give her a call."

"I don't know. I'm not going to be here long enough to get much out of it."

"You might be surprised. Just think about it."

They talked awhile longer, then Carly finished her shopping and left. However, the conversation kept replaying in her mind. Not only the mention of the widow's group but the comments about her and Mack. There had never been anything romantic between them. Oh, when she was younger she'd idolized him, the older boy who helped around the lodge. They'd become friends; at times she'd shown him how to do many of the tasks around the campgrounds.

Later, when she was older, she'd had a crush on him, but she'd gotten over that. Hadn't she? Carly slid behind the wheel of her car. Truthfully, her feelings for Mack had always been complicated. Her attraction and admiration had warred with her resentment and hurt. Her young heart had found him handsome and exciting, but when she'd realized her father seemed to prefer spending time with Mack rather than with her, her feelings turned sour even though she couldn't completely evict him from her heart.

She'd come back that last summer, partly because she had to as a condition of the custody agreement, but she also wanted to see Mack again and sort out her feelings for him. He was the thread tugging her back, and she'd never be free of the lodge unless she could understand her feelings. But her visit had ended in more pain and confusion, and she'd hurried back to her mom and never looked back.

There was nothing left at Longleaf for

her. And the sooner she and Ella returned to Atlanta, the better.

Mack listened to Lucy's prayers, gave her a kiss on the forehead, then tucked the cover in around her little form. "Sweet dreams, pumpkin."

"I love you, Uncle Mack"

"Love you, too."

"Do you think Ella and her mom will stay here a long time? I like having a best friend."

"I don't know, but I hope so, too. Miss Carly was always my best friend."

Lucy smiled up at him, sending a warm ring of happiness that encircled his heart.

Downstairs Mack poured himself a cup of coffee and went outside onto the deck. The weather was staying warmer into the night. May was always the perfect time of year in Mississippi. Not too hot, not too cold.

His gaze lingered on the lake and the reflection of the full moon on the water. He loved it here. He hadn't realized how much until he'd heard the terms of the will and the threat of losing the lodge forever had become a real possibility. If only he could find a way to reconnect Carly with this place.

Out of the corner of his eye, movement drew his attention to the garden swing at the edge of the lake. Something was on the swing? Had an animal curled up on the seat? The shadow moved and he realized the critter was a person. Carly?

Concern lanced through him, and he set the coffee cup aside and hurried across the lawn. The sounds of sobbing reached him as he drew near. Carly never cried. Ever. He halted, considering his next move. Should he speak to her or quietly back away and leave her alone?

Before he could move, Carly glanced up and saw him. The look on her face broke his heart. "You okay?"

She shook her head, then shrugged, then swiped at her eyes.

He persisted. "Do you want some company?"

She shrugged again. And sniffed.

He sat down beside her, waiting for her to speak. He remembered that you couldn't rush Carly. When she was ready to share, she would.

"Was he sick for long?" she asked him.

Mack studied her a moment. Was the lodge starting to penetrate the thick wall of anger? "No. It all happened pretty fast. He got the diagnosis, and two months later he was gone."

"Did you see him?"

"I did. I came up to see him when he was in

the hospital. Wade didn't want anyone to know he was sick. When he went into the hospital, Dwayne thought I should know. He asked to see you."

"He did? I didn't even know he was sick."

"Dwayne called your mother, but she refused to give him your number. He tried to track you down, but he didn't know where to look. The last contact he had was with Troy, but he couldn't locate you that way, either. There were a dozen Troy Hughes in Atlanta."

"Why did he do this?"

"What's that?"

"This crazy will thing. Why not just leave the whole place to you?"

"Why would he do that? You're his daughter. He should have left it all to you."

She shook her head. "No. He always loved you more."

Mack couldn't believe what he was hearing. "What are you talking about? That's the dumbest thing I've ever heard. I was just an employee. You're his only child. He loved you more than anything."

Carly shook her head, pulling herself into a tighter ball. "No. I realized he didn't when I was sixteen. That was the year he chose you over me. It was my sixteenth birthday. We were going to go to a movie and then to dinner. It was our yearly ritual. That year he was going to take me to a fancy place in Hastings. But he went somewhere with you instead."

Mack struggled to remember a time when he and Wade had ever gone to a movie. "No. We never did that."

"I saw you out by the cart shed. You came up to him and said something, and he literally dropped what he was doing and hurried off with you. He patted you on the shoulder and left his arm around you as you walked away. He never came back. I got dressed and waited and waited, but he never came back. My mom was gone—she'd taken a vacation or something—and I really wanted some special time with Dad. But he had chosen you over me. He tried to explain to me later, but I was too upset." She wiped her eyes again. "Mom came back the next day, and she and Dad fought worse than ever. Then we left."

Mack's heart had twisted as he listened. He remembered that day well. "Carly, you're wrong. That wasn't what happened."

Carly looked away.

He wanted to pull her close to comfort her but didn't dare. "I remember that day clearly. I came to your dad for help. I'd gotten a call from my mom's neighbor. She'd found my mom unconscious on the floor. I was terrified. Your dad took me home and stayed with me when the ambulance took Mom to the hospital and stayed there until we knew she was going to be all right. He was helping me, Carly, not choosing me over you."

Mack studied her a moment. She didn't react or speak, so he had no idea what she was thinking. Maybe she didn't believe him. "Your father loved you more than anything. No one could ever take your place. Yes, we were close. He was my mentor and I loved him, but I could never be more important to him than you. Maybe if you'd let him explain what had happened, you would have understood."

"No. It wouldn't have changed anything. Mom came back the next day and told me the truth. Then we left."

"What truth?" There was something more. Something she wasn't telling him, and his instincts told him it had more to with Carly's deep-seated anger than her believing Wade cared more for him than her. Carly remained silent. There was nothing to be gained by hanging around. He stood, resisting the urge to touch her. "I'm sorry you felt that way, but there was no reason to. You were Wade's precious child, and nothing or no one could change that." She didn't respond. "Are you coming inside?"

"Not yet."

"Okay. If you want to talk, you know where to find me."

His heart was heavy as he started back to the lodge. Her confession shone a light on many things that had puzzled him over the years. If he looked at things objectively, he could see where Carly might have misinterpreted his and Wade's relationship. Mack ached for her, all these years believing that her father didn't care.

He glanced back over his shoulder at Carly. She was still huddled in the swing. She looked so sad and alone. He wished she would let him comfort her, be a friend again. He knew one thing for certain. Before she left here, he would make sure she understood how much her father had loved her.

Chapter Four

Carly stopped outside the door of the psychologist's office and inhaled a deep breath. Ashley smiled over at her.

"You're not going to an execution, sweetie. It's only a therapy group."

She grinned and nodded. "I know I'm acting ridiculous, but I'm just not sure how this will help me with the will situation."

"It probably won't. But it might help you in other ways, some you may not even know you need help with."

Carly shook her head. "Now you're just talking nonsense."

Ashley opened the door. "We'll see."

The inner office was a soothing space of muted colors and comfy furniture. Several ladies were already there, helping themselves to soft drinks at a small table near the window.

Carly's anxiety downshifted. Maybe Ash was right. Maybe it would be good to talk to other women who had been through the experience of widowhood.

"Good evening, ladies."

An attractive woman in her thirties entered, a warm smile lighting up her face. Carly had expected a more matronly type, not someone near her age. She made a beeline toward her.

"Carly, right? I'm so glad to meet you and that you decided to come. After our brief phone call the other day, I was afraid I might have scared you off."

"No, not at all. Besides, Ashley has sung your praises and that of the group." She had questioned why she should attend the sessions. Other than the situation with the will, she was doing all right. Ella was completely healed from her heart surgery, she loved her job, she had a nice apartment, and somehow she'd find a way to deal with all the debt hanging over her head. Then Mack had found her on the swing, crying like a two-year-old, and he'd explained about the day her dad had stood her up.

That revelation had turned her world upside down. All her assumptions about her father and his relationship with Mack were suddenly in question. Her dad had tried to tell her why he'd missed her birthday outing, but she'd been so angry and hurt she'd refused to let him explain and hidden in her room to nurse her disappointment.

Nina called the group to order and they settled in. Carly was surprised to find how comfortable the group was. She listened as they each commented on their week. Paula, Charlotte, Jen and Trudy had been with the group a long time. Ashley and a woman named Donna were relatively new. All the women had challenges that they were struggling with in their lives, and each comment touched something deep inside Carly.

When it was her turn to speak, Nina told her she could wait until she felt more comfortable, but something about the women here gave her courage and the security to open up.

"I wasn't sure I wanted to come here. I didn't think I really had anything to work out. My issues are all current and have nothing to do with being a widow. But now I'm wondering if there might be something I'm missing."

Paula chuckled. "She's a quick learner, this one."

The others joined in the teasing.

Charlotte leaned forward. "So what's going on that you wanted to join our group? I think I can speak for all of us when I say we came here for one reason and found out there was something totally different at work."

Carly took a moment to consider her words before offering a quick explanation about her father's quirky will and the resulting complications. "I just want to sell the place and get on with my life."

Trudy pushed her glasses up on her nose. "Are you sure that's what you want?"

"Yes. Of course. I have no good memories of the lodge."

Jen raised her eyebrows. "Really? Whenever I hear a declarative statement like that it sends up red flags, which usually mean the person is in serious denial."

Nina nodded. "Not always, but many times it's a clue as to what's really going on."

Carly shook her heard. "I'm not. I want to sell the lodge and go home. Nothing complicated about that."

"I know I'm new here." Donna scooted forward on the chair. "But I think they may have a point. You say you grew up at this lodge and you have no good memories, not even one. I find that hard to believe. Sounds to me like you're avoiding something."

Caught like a fish on a hook, she stared at her hands a long moment. If she were perfectly honest with herself, she was full of good memories. It was just the few bad ones that had blacked them out. "I suppose there are good memories. The truth is, I need the money from the sale to pay off my daughter's medical bills. She had a serious heart surgery, and the expense was more than my insurance would cover. Way more."

The sympathetic response from the women brought tears to her eyes.

Jen spoke up. "I'm a nurse and I know of some organizations that can help with those kinds of expenses. If you'd like, I can put you touch with them."

"That would be wonderful, thank you."

Paula chuckled. "One problem solved. So what's the next bugaboo you're trying to avoid."

Carly cringed. There was no way she was going to bring up all the issues with Mack. "Not a thing. Thanks to this group I won't even have to come back next week."

Charlotte laughed. "Right. Trust me, you'll find a whole boatload of reasons to come back. I've been coming for years. Paula is one of the original members."

Carly studied the older woman.

Paula grimaced. "Don't look at me that way. This isn't a one-size-fits-all kind of group. I have a lot of issues to work through. Being a widow isn't like having the flu, you know. It's a chronic condition. You never completely recover."

When the meeting ended and Carly was on her way home, she replayed all the comments the women had made. Each had a different story, a different journey, but she'd identified with each of them. The thread of widowhood connected them all.

Pulling up to the lodge, the glow from inside gave the old home a welcoming feeling. She remembered coming home at night and seeing the lights and the sense of being home that had warmed her.

Sometimes she'd enter the living quarters from their side of the porch, other times she'd enter through the main room so she could see all the guests. They always looked so happy and friendly. It made her proud to be the owner, knowing she was partly responsible for their visit to Longleaf.

So how did she allow all the good things to resurface when the last ones marred everything that had come before?

Perhaps the ladies were right. She might have many more reasons to attend the meetings.

Mack watched Carly's car pull up the long lane to the lodge and park at the side where the living quarters were located. Thelma had told him she had a meeting of some sort with a widow's group, but he suspected her motivation was something else entirely. The four of them were supposed to sit down tonight and finalize the priority list of the necessary repairs. It didn't take a psychologist to realize Carly was avoiding making those decisions.

From where he sat on the corner of the wide wraparound porch, he could see Carly as she walked toward the main door. Her gait was slow and labored, as if she was deep in thought. He wished he could ease her sadness somehow. She stopped and stiffened. Mack froze. Had she sensed his presence?

"Mack?"

He inhaled a slow breath. He really didn't want to confront her tonight. "Yeah."

She walked across the porch and stopped a few feet away. "Are you keeping tabs on me?"

He smiled. "No, Carly. I was merely enjoying the warm evening. How was your meeting?"

"Fine. Sorry I wasn't here to talk about the lodge plans. Maybe we can go over everything in the morning."

"No need." He stood. "We went ahead without you. We can't afford to waste any time."

"Why would you do that? I have a say in this, too."

"You do. But you weren't here. Besides, I can fill you in right now. Bottom line is we can't open in a week. There are too many repairs to make and not enough employees available. We've pushed the opening back another week, but even that's doubtful."

Carly rubbed her temple. "But Thelma and Dwayne were so sure we could open quickly."

"That was before we knew the extent of the repairs, and they were working on the assumption that many of the former employees would return to work. I know this has put a crimp in your plans, but it's only a small setback."

Carly shook her head. "No. It's not small at all. At this rate I'll never get back home."

"This is your home, Carly. It always was and always will be. You can deny it, you can lie to yourself from now till the end of time, but you can't run from it."

"You don't know me anymore, Mack." She squared her shoulders and met his gaze. "Whatever was here for me was destroyed long ago, and nothing can repair it. If you'll excuse me, I have to check on my daughter."

"Lucy and Ella are curled up with my tablet watching *Annie*."

Carly grinned. "Which means they'll be singing 'Tomorrow' all day."

"Or 'Hard-Knock Life.'" Mack slipped his hands into his pockets. "Thelma is waiting to talk to you. She wants to do a walk-through of the lodge rooms and take inventory on what needs to be done before we open."

Carly crossed her arms over her chest and set her jaw. "It's late, maybe we can do that in the morning."

Mack grinned. "It's only eight o'clock and there are only ten rooms. You never used to procrastinate. The Carly I remember used to jump in with both feet. Fearless."

"I was a child back then." She turned to go inside, but he moved quickly and opened the door. It was nice to see her fire again. He just wished it was directed toward getting the lodge open and not digging in her heels and trying to avoid things.

Thelma was seated near the fireplace, reading a book, and glanced up as they entered. "Oh, good. You're back. Was it a good meeting?"

Mack was curious about the answer, but Carly merely shrugged. "It was fine. Where's Ella?"

Thelma gestured toward the seating area facing the lake at the far end of the room. Ella and Lucy were huddled together watching the movie. Carly watched them a long moment before turning away.

"Mack said you wanted to do a quick inventory of the rooms?"

"Yes. We need to utilize every moment if we're going to pull this off. Let me get my checklist and I'll be right back."

Mack saw her shoulders tense, then ease as she turned her gaze toward her daughter again. He took a step closer, too close, the light scent of her floral perfume in the air. "Your daughter has been a real blessing to Lucy. Having a friend right now is helping her more than you can imagine. If nothing else comes from your time at the lodge, maybe you can take comfort knowing that Ella has helped Lucy."

"I'm glad. Ella has needed a friend, as well. She's been through a lot."

He could sense there was something significant behind her words, but she looked away. Now was not the time. "Then coming home wasn't a complete waste, was it?"

Before she could answer, Thelma returned with a clipboard. "This shouldn't take long. The lodge has been closed only a couple of months. There should only be small things to attend to."

Mack took the opportunity to inject his opinion. "We need to talk in the morning, Carly. I'll go over the list of repairs on the property. Dwayne and I have made a preliminary list, but you need to look at it, too. We can save time if we're all on the same page."

She nodded and walked away. Mack watched her go, wishing he could do something to ease her concern and wondering why the money was suddenly so important to her. She'd never been the type. He had to assume that her mother had converted her, and now that she'd seen what the big city had to offer she wasn't content with the simple life at the lodge.

Even as the thought formed, he couldn't accept it. There was something missing. Something had happened that he didn't know about. He prayed he could crack her shell before it was too late and she walked out of his life again.

Carly took the stairs to her room with a sense of relief. The inventory of the guest rooms had produced a short repair list. Two rooms needed holes repaired in the wall, the air-conditioning unit in another was not functioning, and two others required carpet cleaning. Overall, things were in good shape. Carly had hoped to freshen up the rooms with new bedding and curtains, but Thelma informed her that the bulk of the budget had to be used for the grounds.

Carly unlocked her room and stepped inside. Turning on the light, she was struck by how empty the room felt. Without Ella in the bed next to hers, the room was devoid of warmth and life. When the movie had ended, Lucy had asked Ella to sleep over in her room tonight. Carly had started to say no, but the look of bright hope in her daughter's eyes changed her mind. She couldn't deny her the excitement of a sleepover with a new friend. Ella had spent too many nights in a hospital bed with no one to comfort her but a nurse. After all, she'd still be under the same roof, only a few rooms down the hallway.

After Mack's comments about the closeness the girls had developed, she didn't want to deny either of them special times together. This trip might be difficult for her, but it didn't have to be for Ella.

Her cell phone rang just as she was climbing into bed. The name on the screen caused her heart to race. Her mother. These conversations never went well and, Lord forgive her, she was thankful that her mom rarely called. "Hi, Mom. Everything all right up there in

Maine?" She tried to keep her voice pleasant and friendly.

"It rained today. I hate rain. But Sanford took me to the ballet tonight, so that was lovely. I had a new gown to wear."

"That's nice, Mom. I'm happy for you."

"Where are you, Carly Anne? That woman you work for wouldn't tell me."

Carly took a second to calm herself. Her mother insisted on calling Carly's boss, Jessie Duncan, 'that woman.' "I'm in Hastings, Mom, at the lodge."

"Why are you there? You have no reason to visit that backwoods hut."

"Dad left it to me in his will."

"Why would he do that? He knew you wanted no part of that debacle."

"I'm his only heir." No need to mention the complication of Mack's involvement. "I have to settle the estate."

"I suggest you deal with it quickly and get home. No good can come from you hanging around the lake again. Honestly, none of this would have happened if Richard had been where he was supposed to."

Carly frowned. "Who's Richard?"

"Who?"

"You said Richard."

"I most certainly did not. I said Wade. We were talking about your father."

Carly pressed her lips together. Ever since her mother had suffered a fall last year that had resulted in a severe concussion, her memory was spotty and often times she'd make statements that made no sense at all. "I need to go, Mom. It's late and I want to get to bed. There's a lot to do here."

"Of course, dear. Just get done quickly. Give Ella a hug for me."

"I will."

Carly ended the call and plugged in her phone to charge, laying it on the nightstand. It would take her a while to fall to sleep now. Her mother's call had dredged up silt from the past and the residue would float around in her mind for hours. Tonight she would be sorting through her memories for someone named Richard. Who was he and what did he have to do with her family?

The morning sun woke Carly early, streaming across the covers and warming the room. She rose and went to the window. The lake was beautiful. Ripples on the water sparkled in the sunlight. The view from this room was the best in the lodge. But there was another that was equally spectacular—the view from her parents' room in the apartment.

She turned away from the window. It was time to face a few realities. If they were going to open the lodge, then she couldn't take up space in the best room. Like it or not, she and Ella would have to move into her parents' apartment. As much as she hated to admit it, it was best for Ella to have a home to stay in instead of a hotel room.

She'd speak with Thelma this morning and move in as soon as possible. After getting dressed in shorts and a T-shirt, she hurried downstairs, anxious to be there when Ella and Lucy appeared.

They padded into the kitchen just as she was pouring a cup of coffee. They looked so cute in their oversize T-shirts and tousled hair. Ella came to her for a hug and Lucy sought out Thelma.

"Did you have fun at your sleepover?"

Ella nodded a big smile. "Can Lucy stay in our room tonight?"

"We'll see. I have a lot to do today."

"Can we walk on the trail? Lucy said there is a cool one here."

Lucy's eyes lit up. "It's really awesome. It has steps and a creek, and there's a bridge, too."

Carly recognized the description. It was the

Piney Woods Trail. "Sure. That would be fun. Lucy can come, too."

Thelma smiled, scooped two cinnamon rolls onto plates and set them in front of the girls.

Carly couldn't miss the joy on the woman's face. "I think you like playing grandma."

Thelma nodded. "I do. They are both so sweet and so much fun."

Mack strode into the kitchen. "I thought I smelled Thelma's cinnamon rolls." He smiled at Carly. "Thank you for letting Ella spend the night with Lucy."

"I hope they didn't keep you up."

He shook his head. "A few fits of giggles but nothing I couldn't handle."

Thelma handed him a plate with two large rolls. "Dwayne ran into the marina for some supplies. He said we could meet as soon as he gets back. Or you can fill Carly in to save time."

Mack nodded and took a seat at the counter. "Okay. Most of this you already know. The short version is we have five canoes needing repairs. Two of the cabins are in good shape and just need cleaning. The other three need various repairs like plumbing, electrical and a new roof." He took a sip of his coffee, avoiding her gaze. "And as you saw, the big cabin needs major repairs."

Her mind leaped ahead to other areas needing work. "What about the camper lots and the RV pads?"

"Minor attention needed, mainly turning on power. The pool and snack bar need cleaning and inspections."

"How long will that take?"

"Several days, depending on when we can get the help."

"What about the trails?"

"They're littered with limbs and debris, but we need to get the cabin repairs underway first."

Carly's hope began to rise. She'd been dejected when the first week had passed with very little being accomplished. Between settling in and adjusting to being back at the lodge, she'd avoided getting drawn into the projects. From here on, she'd make sure things got done. There was very little about running the lodge and campgrounds she didn't know. She'd roll up her sleeves and tackle whatever needed to be done. No more delays.

"Great. Then I'll see what I can do to help with the cabins and tackle the trails after that."

Mack looked at her over the rim of his cup. "Can't wait to get your hands dirty, huh?"

Carly took a sip of her coffee. "Can't wait to put up a for-sale sign."

Thelma waved them off. "Y'all go ahead. I'll watch the girls. Most of what I have to do is over the phone or on the computer."

Mack stood. "I'll be out front with the golf cart in five. If you're not there, you'll have to walk to the cabins."

Carly bit her bottom lip. Why had she said that? She knew it would upset him. She glanced at Thelma, who was looking at her with raised brows. "I know. I shouldn't have said that about the sale, but he wants me to feel something here and I just can't."

"Can't or won't? I understand why you feel the way you do. Those last years were painful, but before that you were happy here. Every day you would bounce into this kitchen full of excitement about what you were going to do around the grounds. Can't you try and remember those times and not the others?"

"I'll try. And I'll start by moving our things into the apartment. I don't want to tie up a guest room that could be used for paying visitors."

"You and Mack think alike. He and Lucy are moving in with us for the same reason. With our place just up the way he'll be close enough to help out, but not take up space at the lodge."

The statement brought back an old memory from before her parents' divorce. There were times when she and Mack would read each other's thoughts. They were both so attuned to the campground and what needed to be done that they often meet up each morning with the same tasks in mind. Apparently, that hadn't changed.

Chapter Five

Mack was ready to pull away from the lodge when Carly came out of the door. She hurried toward him, bringing a smile to his face he didn't bother to hide. She looked like she did years ago in shorts, a cotton shirt and her hair pulled into a ponytail. A much shorter one than when she was a teen but still cute and sassy.

She swung into the cart and propped one foot on the dash, tossing him a challenging look. "You waiting for an invitation?"

He offered a quick salute and drove off.

"What's on the work schedule today?"

"New roof on cabin two. Contrary to what you might think, Dwayne and I have removed the old shingles and installed half of the new ones. Just need to finish that, then we can move on to the next task on the list."

"Which is?"

"Hire contractors to do the electrical and plumbing repairs."

"I thought Dwayne was a licensed contractor?"

"He is but only for carpentry work. He has to subcontract out the electrical and plumbing. They'll start work tomorrow."

"Good. Sounds like things are finally moving forward."

"That should make you very happy." He pulled to a stop near the middle cabin and got out. He had no idea why Carly was here unless it was to supervise his work and make sure he kept up a steady clip. He put on his nail apron and tool belt, then walked to the stack of shingles and hoisted one onto his shoulder. When he turned around, Carly was topping the ladder and stepping onto the roof.

"What are you doing?"

"Helping."

"You're going to nail shingles?"

"It won't be the first time."

Mack had a flashback to the Carly he remembered. She'd never backed away from hard work, and she'd often matched her dad job for job even as a teen. "Fine. But you might want to go back and change those shorts for a pair of jeans. Your knees won't last ten minutes."

She leaned slightly forward and scanned the

ground. "Toss me those knee pads, then I'll be good to go."

One thing he hadn't forgotten about his old friend was that once she made up her mind, you might as well go along. Dumping the shingle bundle back onto the stack, he tossed the knee pads up, then picked up Dwayne's nail apron and a hammer before hoisting the bundle again and starting up the ladder.

Carly quickly took the apron, pads and hammer, and fitted herself for work. Mack placed the shingles between them. "You have a utility knife in that apron?"

She grinned and held it up. "Where do I start?"

"Continue with the lower course. I'll pick up the row in the middle and you can start the next row. That way we won't get in each other's way."

Carly pulled several shingles from the pile and carried them to the side of the roof, laying them out and reaching for her hammer and a handful of roofing nails.

"Be sure and line up the rain slots properly."

She gave him a long, icy glare. "I know how to do this."

He raised his hands in submission, grinning inwardly. "I wasn't sure you'd remember how. You seem to have forgotten most of what you learned here." He wanted to bite his tongue as soon as the words were spoken.

"I might be a little rusty, but it'll come back to me. Just like riding a bike."

They worked silently as the courses of shingles slowly moved up the roof.

Carly took a break, sitting on the roof and taking a swig of water. "I would have thought Dwayne would have a nail gun for this kind of job."

Mack swung his hammer again and wiped his brow. "He does. It's being repaired so we're doing this the old-fashioned way."

"Dad always talked about putting tin roofs on the cabins. He thought it would be a nice touch for the guests. Guess he changed his mind."

"No. He just didn't have the money after the divorce."

"What do you mean? He always found money for the campgrounds."

Mack sat back on his heels, wishing he'd learn to measure his words before he spoke. "He could barely keep the place afloat after the divorce settlement. He nearly lost the business at one point."

"I don't understand. Mom always complained that he wasn't paying his share, that he was always behind on support payments. We didn't have enough to live on."

She met his gaze and he could see the doubts and questions swirling in her brown eyes. Was it possible that she didn't know how much Wade had to fork over each month to his ex?

"Did he discuss family matters with you?"

Mack shook his head. "No. Never. Though he said things here and there, and it was obvious that the upgrades he normally did each year weren't happening. It was three years before he could get back on track."

Carly stared off into the distance. "That's when my mom remarried," she muttered softly.

"And the alimony stopped." Once again Mack wished he'd held his tongue. Carly turned away and went back to work finishing the top course of shingles, pounding in each nail with more force than necessary. He was usually so good at keeping his thoughts to himself, but now being around Carly loosened his tongue and widened the gap between them. Mack set to work putting the ridge cap on the top of the cabin. He hated the notion that Carly believed her dad was a deadbeat.

With the roofing complete, Mack slid his hammer into his tool belt and dropped the excess shingle scraps onto the ground before looking at Carly. She'd sat down on the roof again and was staring out at the lake. "Another job crossed off the list."

She nodded and stood before carefully approaching the ladder. "A drop in the bucket."

Mack stepped ahead of her and swung around onto the first rung. "I'll go first. Just in case."

She gave him a frosty glare. "I know how to go down a ladder."

Safely on the ground, Mack held the side of the metal ladder while Carly made her way down. On the next to the last step, her foot slipped, dropping her to the ground. He caught her around the waist, his heart pounding. "You all right?"

She nodded before turning to look at him. Her fawn-colored eyes were wide with alarm. "I misjudged the rung."

"It happens. That's why I was here, to catch you in case you fell." It's where he always wanted to be, but he'd have to accept the fact that it would never happen. He told himself to step away and let her move off, but he liked the sensation of her being in his arms.

Suddenly she broke eye contact and gently elbowed him back. "So what's next? We still have half a day."

Before he could respond, Dwayne drove up in his truck, pulling a large flat trailer. He waved out the window. "Roof looks good. Did you help, Carly?"

She gave him a thumbs-up.

He grinned. "Good to know you still have your skills."

"What's the trailer for?"

"I ran into George Meacham at the marina, and he said if we can get the canoes to him today he'd put them at the top of his to-do list. Y'all want to give me a hand?"

Mack nodded and glanced at Carly. She took a step back and gestured toward the ground.

"I'll pick up around here."

Mack climbed into Dwayne's truck and a let out a slow breath, welcoming the chance to put some distance between him and Carly. His senses were still reeling from being so close. He needed to get a handle on his emotions. Fast, before he did something stupid.

Working alongside her had felt like old times. Only they weren't. This was a different time and they were different people. They could never go back to those young people who were so close.

But, oh, how he wished they could.

Carly watched the truck pull away, finally exhaling the breath that had been trapped in her lungs. What in the world had just happened? She'd been determined to jump into the repairs to make sure things moved quickly. It had felt good to channel all her anger into driving the nails into the roof. Then she'd slipped on the ladder and ended up in Mack's arms, close enough to feel the heat from his body and inhale his scent. She should have shoved him away, but instead she'd lingered, feeling her pulse speed up, her heart pound and her every sense vibrate to his nearness. It was insane.

And dangerous.

She pivoted and reached down to pick up the paper wrapping from the shingle bundles. There was no reason to flip out over her reaction to Mack. It was a onetime thing, an anomaly. A moment of weakness triggered by old memories of something that would never happen again.

Carly focused on picking up the roofing debris and placing the tools in the back of the golf cart. As she was finishing up, Dwayne's truck reappeared, the long trailer stacked with silver canoes. Mack got out. Carly took a closer look at the water craft, then leaned in the truck window. "These are all pretty banged up."

Dwayne tilted his hat upward a tad. "A couple of them were already needing work from normal use, but several of them were tossed pretty hard in that storm a while back."

"How long will it take to get them operational?"

"Less than a week, I hope."

Carly sighed. "Well, at least we have two that are intact for when we open."

Dwayne pulled away and Carly tried to ignore Mack, who was standing beside her. She was thankful that her phone rang, until she saw the name on the screen. The collection agency again. Her heart chilled. She'd avoided them for over a week. She'd learned the hard way that if she didn't answer, it only made things worse the next time.

"I have to take this." She couldn't risk looking at Mack. She walked off a few paces and answered the call. The voice on the other end launched into a stern dialogue, tinged with more threats and stating that they were taking steps to garnishee her wages. Carly's throat tightened. "I'm doing the best I can. My father died recently and I have to deal with his estate. Maybe we can work something out when I get back home."

The voice wasn't interested in making any deals, only getting a payment. Today. A scream worked its way up through her and Carly ended the call, resisting the urge to toss the phone into the bushes. Instead, she jammed it into her pocket as the tears started to roll down her cheeks.

"Carly. Is everything okay?" Mack came to her side.

Keeping her back to him, she wiped the tears. "Fine." She schooled her features and turned to face him. She tried to ignore the look of concern on Mack's face, but the tenderness in his probing blue gaze was too much. Her usual determination started to crumble. "No. Nothing is all right. Everything is falling apart and I don't know how to stop it."

Mack took her arm and led her to the picnic table in front of the cabin and sat down. "What's going on? Maybe I can help."

"No. The only thing that will help is selling this place."

"Who was that on the phone, Carly? What upset you so?"

She weighed her options. She didn't really want to tell Mack but, then, what did she have to lose? She was at her wit's end. Her pride was the least of her worries now. "Bill collectors. They hound me day and night."

"Why. What happened?"

"Ella's surgery."

"I don't understand. Was she sick?"

Carly clasped her hands, rubbing her thumbs together. "She was born with a serious and rare heart condition. It couldn't be repaired until she was older. The surgery was six months ago."

"Is she okay now?"

"She's perfect. Completely normal. I don't have to worry about her at all. She's so happy and so excited to be able to do everything other kids do. But the surgery was very expensive and my insurance only covered a fraction of the cost."

Mack nodded and rubbed his jaw. "Is that why you're so anxious to sell the lodge? To pay off the hospital bills?"

"They are threatening to garnishee my wages. I'm barely making it week to week as it is. I owe more than I can ever pay." She propped her elbows on the top of the picnic table. "I've been battling financial trouble since Troy died. He was a wonderful husband and father, but he made some bad investments and we lost everything. When he died, Ella and I were left with only enough for his funeral. We managed until the surgery but now—"

Mack gently touched her shoulder. "I wish I could help."

She stared at her hands. "I just wish they'd stop calling me. I'm doing the best I can."

Mack leaned closer. "Maybe I can help a little."

"How?"

"It's against the law for collection agencies

to harass you. They're rarely prosecuted, so they ignore the law. But I'm an attorney."

She met his gaze. "I thought you were a deputy."

A corner of Mack's mouth lifted. "I am, but I do have my law degree. I just never took the bar exam. I can't officially do anything, but I can send a strongly worded and very official sounding letter reminding them of the law and threatening legal action."

"Will they stop calling me?"

"For a while. At least until things here are sorted out."

The thought of not freezing up each time a bill collector showed up on her phone gave her hope. "Thank you. But if you're not licensed, can you really do this?"

"You'd be amazed how the word *lawyer* can strike fear in the hearts of evildoers everywhere."

Carly smiled, the sense of panic fading away. She reached over and took his hand. "Thank you."

He laid his other hand over hers, encasing her in a warm sense of security. "Why didn't you tell me why the money was so important? I would have understood."

"There's was nothing you could have done. It's too much money for anyone to pay back."

She wiped her eyes again. "One of the ladies at the widow's group I went to knows of
an organization that can help people in situa-
tions like mine."

"Good. I'll help you talk to them if you like."

"Thank you. Sometimes I get so tired of
doing everything by myself."

He put his arm around her shoulders and
drew her close, letting her rest her head on his
chest. "We'll work this out, Carly. I promise."

She fought the desire to remain forever in
his embrace. It felt good to lean on someone,
to share her burden. But his offer to help her
with the medical situation didn't change all the
other things she was facing. Even with help,
the end result was that bills needed to be paid
and the lodge needed to be sold.

She pushed away, trying to ignore the solid
feel of his chest.

He stood. "I'm starving. Why don't we take
a break and get some lunch?"

"I am hungry, but it'll have to be quick. I'm
moving our things into the apartment this afternoon. We need all the lodge rooms free for
guests."

Mack stood. "Moving back home, huh?"

She shrugged. "I think Ella will be happier
in the house instead of a guest room."

Mack slid behind the wheel of the golf cart

and waited for her to be seated before starting the vehicle. "I understand. That's why Lucy and I are moving in with the Thompsons. They have plenty of room and I think the environment of a real house will be good for Lucy. Not to mention having live-in grandparents."

"They do seem to be enjoying the girls."

"Another reason to be thankful for coming home. You've made them happy."

"I suppose." That's not something she'd considered, but he had a point. Dwayne and Thelma were genuinely delighted to have everyone back at the lodge.

They rode in silence until they reached the lodge. Mack pulled to a stop near the back entrance. "Carly, maybe you should stop being so stubborn and just admit that you have good memories of the lodge and your dad."

Carly set her jaw and got out of the cart. "You don't know what you're talking about. And I'd appreciate it if everyone would stop trying to make me remember things I don't want to relive." Pivoting on her heel, she walked away.

The knot that had formed in Mack's stomach since Carly had come home tightened. Everything he said to her triggered her anger and resentment. He was at his wit's end to know how to approach her anymore.

Maybe she had the right idea after all. The obstacles were mounting more than he or the Thompsons had anticipated. He was beginning to think getting the lodge open was an impossible task. If he agreed to sell, then it would all be done. He could go back home to the coast, raise Lucy and let any ideas about Carly slowly die away.

He rubbed his forehead. Except he knew that would never happen. Seeing her again and being close had only unearthed all the feelings he'd carried for her from the first day they'd met.

Steering the cart back toward the shed, he caught sight of Lucy and Ella playing with the puppies in the backyard. They each held a furry pet in their arms, their smiles revealing their delight. He doubted the poor dogs' feet had touched the ground since the girls had met them. They carried the critters everywhere.

He stopped and took a closer look at Ella, his heart stinging as he thought about what she and her mother must have been through. He couldn't imagine dealing with something so serious. Lucy was his life now, and the thought of her needing major surgery filled him with fear and dread. How had Carly managed all alone? He'd always known she was a strong and determined woman, but it would have taken an extra measure of courage to deal with a seriously ill child.

He drove on, his thoughts still occupied with the things Carly had shared. The one that lingered was the tone in her voice when she spoke of her husband. It was clear she'd adored him. Losing him at such a young age must have been devastating. He wished he could have been there to comfort her through the loss and the anxious days of Ella's surgery. But he doubted he could have lived up to the man she married.

His cell phone rang as he was leaving the shed. His concern spiked when he saw it was from the prison. Val only called once a week. Something must be wrong. He answered and held his breath.

"Hey, little bro."

"Val, is everything okay?"

"Not really. I'm in the infirmary. I got into a little scuffle and broke my arm."

Mack knew enough about the prison system to read between the lines. Beatings were a common problem among inmates. "Are you going to be all right?"

"Sure. I just wanted to let you know and see how my baby is doing."

"She's happy. She loves it here at the lodge, and she and Ella are best buds."

"I'm glad. Look, I don't have much time so I want you to think about something. I'd like you to adopt Lucy. Straight out."

The request hit like a blow to his chest. He fought to find his voice. "Val. I can't do that. She's your daughter."

"And she'll be seventeen when and if I get out of here, and I'll be a stranger to her. I want her to have a normal life with a loving parent. That's you."

"Val. You understand that means you'd have to relinquish all your parental rights forever."

"I know. But it would be for the best."

Mack's mind was churning. "Sis, you need to reconsider this idea. I'm not sure you're thinking clearly."

"I'm not going to change my mind."

A prerecorded beep sounded, signaling the call was ending.

"We'll talk again. Love you, Val."

The call ended and Mack shoved his phone into his pocket, then walked to the water's edge and leaned against the trunk of an old pine tree." His sister's request was out of the question and he had no idea how to approach her request.

"A man only stares at the water for two reasons. He's either crazy in love or thinking over a problem. Which is it?"

Mack smiled and faced Dwayne, who stopped beside him. "Take a guess."

"Knowing you the way I do, I'd say it's a little of both."

"I hope I'm as wise and all knowing as you are when I'm your age."

"Age has its benefits."

Mack shifted and leaned his back against the tree trunk. "Val wants me to adopt Lucy. She thinks it would be better for her since she'll be a teenager before Val is released."

"Are you open to that idea?"

"I don't know. I'd feel like I was stealing her child. Being her guardian is one thing, but cutting Val out of her life altogether is something else. Lucy would be deeply hurt."

"Maybe. But her mother isn't part of her life right now. You are. And from what I've seen, she is thriving under your care. Her mother is only a once-a-week voice on the phone."

"I don't know. It just doesn't feel right."

"You don't have to decide today. Let it percolate in your mind and heart awhile and have a few long talks with the Lord. You'll find the answer soon enough."

He had other things he was already struggling to sort out. "Did you know Ella had heart surgery a while back?"

"No, I didn't. She okay now?"

Mack nodded. "But the medical bills were staggering. It's why she wants to sell the property."

"Does this mean you're going to change your mind and let the place go?"

Mack pushed away from the tree. "No. Not without looking at every other option first."

Wade had loved Longleaf, and Mack wouldn't stop trying to save it until all solutions were exhausted. In the meantime, he'd try his best to help Carly with her problems, too.

Ella inhaled slowly, her eyes wide, her mouth in a perfect O. "Is this my new room? It's so big." She darted toward the large window. "I can see the whole lake."

Carly set the suitcase and backpack on the bed and smiled at her daughter's delight. She'd felt the same way about the room when she was a child. "This was my room when I was little. I loved the window seat. It's a great place to read a book."

"I love it. I can't wait for Lucy to see it. We're going to have so much fun here."

She had no doubt. The girls were growing closer by the moment. Anyone who saw them might assume they were sisters. "I'm sure you will."

Carly spent the rest of the afternoon getting settled into her childhood home and answering an endless stream of questions from her daughter, many of which forced her to revisit her childhood and her relationship with her father.

She was grateful when bedtime rolled around. Carly tucked Ella into bed and placed a kiss on her head. "Sleep tight, sweetie."

"Mommy, can we stay here forever? I love it here. And I love my friend Lucy."

"I'm glad you're having a good time."

"And I love Miss Thelma, too. Is she my grandma?"

"No. Your grandma, my mom, lives far away. That's why you don't see her." The truth was that she was too busy with her social life to find time to visit her daughter and grandchild.

"Can I pretend Miss Thelma is my grandma?"

"I think she'd like that."

Carly made her way downstairs to the living room of the apartment and opened her laptop. Her boss had emailed her and she'd yet to respond. She had a bad feeling that Jessie would have to let her go. She was supposed to be in Hastings for only a week, two at the most, but it was obviously going to take much longer. But if she lost her job, she'd be destitute.

Tapping the keys, she opened her email, then changed her mind. Speaking to her boss directly might be a better approach. She tried to quell her anxiety as she waited for Jessie to answer. Jessie's voice was filled with concern when she did.

"Are you okay? What's happening over there?"

Reluctantly, Carly explained the situation. "I'm so sorry. I have to stay until the end of next month or until we sell the place. I had no idea this would happen. I was thinking I could still do the ordering and anything that could be done on the computer."

"Well, actually, I've already been working on a plan. I can hire a store manager with no problem. What I really need now is someone to work on marketing and handle social media. A virtual assistant. You're really good at that, Carly. How would you feel about focusing on that end of things while you're gone? I'll keep your pay the same and you can do all your work from Hastings. When you get back, we can assess things and figure out where to go from there?"

Carly wanted to cry with relief. "Thank you, Jessie. That would be perfect. In fact, I'm already starting to work on promoting the lodge, hoping to attract a buyer."

"See. We think alike. I'll get you the links and info you need first thing in the morning."

After discussing her concerns about the lodge, Carly ended the conversation and sent up a prayer of thanks. With the help from the organization Jen had told her about and Mack's offer, she might be able to breathe without thinking about losing everything.

Relief bubbled up and filled her senses. She went out onto the porch and stared out at the lake. The sight melted away much of her animosity and left her with a sweet memory of how much she loved the lodge and the life here. Watching the lake had always soothed her, grounded her, and it was starting to do that now. Maybe Mack was right. She should stop resisting so much and let the good memories resurface.

"Beautiful, isn't it?"

She whirled around to find Mack standing on the ground looking up at her. Words refused to form. He looked so handsome in the moonlight. His blue eyes held an appreciative sparkle and his smile added another degree of warmth to the night air. "Yes. It is. I'd forgotten how lovely." She braced for a snide comment, but he only stepped closer to the deck railing, grasping it with his hands and smiling up at her.

"I'm glad you're starting to remember. I know you won't ever feel the way you used to. I can't expect you to. Too much has happened, but…"

"But what, Mack?"

"I hope you'll leave here without the hate and anger you brought with you and take only the good memories away, for your sake and Ella's."

His words pierced her heart unexpectedly and she leaned against the post. "I don't know if I can. I'm not sure the good ones can overcome the bad."

"Can you tell me what happened? I never understood. It was like everything blew up for no reason. I knew your folks were having trouble, but then all of a sudden your mom left, then she came back and you both left, and nothing was ever the same. Why?"

Carly weighed her options. If she told Mack the truth, his image of her dad would be shattered forever. If she didn't, he'd always be studying her, trying to figure her out, and she didn't think she could live with that for the duration of this situation. She set her jaw and faced him. "Because my dad cheated on my mom. Repeatedly, and she couldn't take it anymore."

Mack's brows drew together and deep creases furrowed his forehead. "No. I don't believe that." He took the steps to the deck and stopped beside her.

Tears stung the back of her eyes, but she blinked them away. She hadn't wanted to believe it, either. "My father wasn't the good guy everyone believed he was."

"No. You're wrong." He took a step back and ran a hand down the back of his neck. "Wade was the most honorable man I ever knew. He loved you and your mom. He would never be unfaithful. It wasn't in his DNA."

"Really? I have proof."

"What kind of proof?"

"An earring left in his truck and it wasn't my mother's."

"How could you know that?"

"It was a clip-on and she had pierced ears."

Mack set his hands on his hips. "What does that prove?"

"There was another woman in my dad's truck. My mom was right. He was seeing someone else."

Mack shook his head and held up a hand as if to ward off the bad news. "No. I don't believe it. He loved your mother. He never had a bad word to say about her. Even when things were heating up at the end, he always took the blame."

"Because he was guilty."

"Not in the way you mean. He'd blame himself for not making more money and for not being able to give her what she wanted."

Carly glanced away. "He refused to find a house in town where Mom would be happy. She wanted a home, and she wanted to have a life and friends that didn't involve strangers. She wanted sidewalks and neighbors, not pine trees and canoes."

"And what was your father going to do for a living if he sold the campgrounds?"

"I don't know." She'd never considered that. Why hadn't she?

"Exactly. Did you even think about that? Your father grew up here He turned this place into a thriving business and provided a good living for his family."

Carly waved his comment away. "You don't understand."

"I think it's *you* who don't understand. You're wrong about your dad. All you have is an earring. You don't know who it belonged to or why it was in the truck. You don't know if it belonged to some sweet young thing that your dad was attracted to or an elderly church lady he drove home on Sunday. Don't you think you should find out before you condemn him?"

"I might've known you'd take his side. You worshipped him."

"So did you."

He was right. She had adored her father, which had made the truth even harder to bear. She started to defend herself, but Mack turned and retraced his steps down to the yard. At the edge of the drive, he glanced back.

"Carly, maybe you should find the truth. I don't know what went on, but I know Wade and I know that isn't something he would do. You're not a kid anymore. Maybe you should take a closer look. With an adult perspective."

She turned away and went inside the lodge. Mack didn't understand. No one did. Her dad had been her hero, her knight in shining armor. To learn that he had feet of clay went far deeper than simple disappointment. It had struck at the core of her belief system and her love. At the time she'd been secretly glad when Mom had dragged her away from the lodge, and she could shove the whole thing to the back of her mind and start fresh.

Inside her kitchen she poured a glass of tea, then wandered out into the lodge. The Thompsons were gone for the evening, the large room empty. The silence settled heavily on her shoulders. Her dad was gone, the guests were gone, and soon the lodge itself would be gone.

Her heart clenched. Was that really what she wanted? To see someone else running Longleaf? Or watch it being bulldozed for a sleek upscale resort hotel?

The thought spiraled downward like a rusty screw into her spirit. But she had to remember the real reason she needed to be free of the lodge. There was no other way to get the kind of money she needed to pay off the hospital bills.

She had to face the fact that letting go wasn't going to be as easy as she'd hoped.

Chapter Six

Mack strode away from the lodge late the next morning, heading toward the lake. The water always calmed him when he was troubled. It's one of the things he liked about living on the coast. After his conversation with Carly last night, he had enough trouble to fill the lake twice over. Without thinking, he made his way to the swing under the live oak at the water's edge and sat down. When he was younger he used to wonder why Carly spent so much time on the swing. Until he'd discovered how soul soothing the movement and the view could be to his troubled spirits.

He started the swing moving, his thoughts replaying his conversation with Carly yesterday. Everything in him rebelled against the idea that Wade had been unfaithful. The man had been a mentor, a surrogate father and his moral compass for half his life. He'd taught him about life, the Lord, the lodge and a myriad of things in between that he used every day.

Wade was a strong Christian man, and Mack found it impossible to believe that he would betray his beliefs by cheating on his wife. Carly had to be wrong.

"Uncle Mack."

He turned as Lucy came racing across the lawn toward him. They'd spent last evening getting settled into the Thompsons' house just a short way up from the lodge. He'd been concerned about intruding on their home, but the floor plan allowed for him and Lucy to have one side of the house to themselves. Thelma insisted on taking care of meals and Mack didn't argue.

Lucy loved the room she was in and promptly rearranged things to her liking.

Thelma had various craft projects planned for the girls every day. She was reveling in the grandma role.

"Hey, little princess." He hugged her close as she climbed up beside him.

"I made you something. Ella and I made them for the people we love most, which is you. Ella made one for her mom. Thelma showed us how."

She handed him a folded piece of red construction paper with a heart drawn on the front. "Open it."

Lucy wiggled with excitement. Mack unfolded the paper, and a heart covered in glitter and lace and tiny flower stickers popped up. He grinned. Lucy was always surprising him with little expressions of love, and he never felt more grateful for her presence in his life than when she did. "It's beautiful. Maybe you could make one for your mom and we could mail it to her."

The smile on Lucy's face quickly faded. "I'll do it later." She rested her head on his arm. "Do you think Ella's mom will like her card as much as you liked mine?"

"I do." Was his niece starting to lose her connection to her mother? How long before she didn't wait eagerly for the weekly phone call? What was his role in her life now?

"Good, 'cause I like Ella and her mom. Don't you? Isn't it nice that God put them in the lodge for us to be friends with?"

"Very nice."

"Uncle Mack, would it be okay with you if I started calling you Daddy?"

A lump lodged in his throat. Was it possible to be touched and concerned at the same time. He chose his words carefully. "But I'm not your daddy, sweetheart. I'm your uncle."

"I know, but I love you like a daddy so why can't I call you that?"

He hugged her to his side, resting his cheek on her head. "How about we think it over for a little while?"

"Deal." Lucy scooted off the swing and waved. "I'm going to find Ella. Can we go fishing later?"

"We'll see. Maybe in a few days. I have lots of work to do at the cabins first."

Mack fingered the pretty card Lucy had made for him, opening and closing it several times and smiling at the way the heart with all its embellishments popped up like a flag. If only he could get Carly's memories to pop up as easily. Given what she'd told him, he was more discouraged than ever. She truly believed her father had been unfaithful. It was a notion that Mack could never accept.

He couldn't say for a fact that Wade hadn't wandered. While he adored the man and had learned many valuable life lessons from his teaching, he didn't know the man. He knew the father figure, the boss, the mentor. They never discussed his personal life or feelings. It would have been inappropriate.

There was one person he could go to for the

truth, though he wasn't sure he'd be willing to share personal information. Mack stood and walked along the lake edge toward the work shed, tucked back in the trees out of sight to preserve the beauty of the landscape.

He found Dwayne at the workbench. He glanced up with a smile. "What you up to, fella?"

"I have some things on my mind."

Dwayne chuckled. "That's never good." He wiped his hands on a rag, then gestured toward the colored paper in Mack's hand. "What ya got there?"

Mack approached him, handing him the card. "Lucy made it for me. She and Ella have been doing crafts with Thelma."

"You do know that my wife has shirked some of her duties around here because she'd rather play grandma to those girls."

"And loving every minute."

"I've never seen her happier. So what got your thoughts all tumbling like crawfish in a boiling pot?"

"I spoke with Carly last night. She told me the reason her parents got divorced was because Wade cheated on her mom more than once. She found an earring in Wade's truck, and she believes it's proof that her dad was unfaithful. I can't believe he'd do that, but I know I'm not aware of the whole situation."

Dwayne leaned a hip against the counter. "Her mother believed he was cheating. She threw it in his face every chance she got. But, no, I don't believe Wade cheated. Despite their issues, he loved her, and he honored his vows."

Mack started to speak, but Dwayne held up his hand. "But I wouldn't swear to that on a stack of Bibles."

"But you just said…"

"No one knows another person completely. He could have had an affair and I wouldn't have known about it. The man I knew was too honorable, too strong in his faith to be unfaithful."

"So what happened? Why is Carly so quick to believe the worst of her dad?"

"I can't answer that. She was just a teen. She probably didn't see things the way they really were. Maybe in time she'll gain a better perspective."

Dwayne patted his back. "In the meantime you need something to keep your mind off your troubles. Let's see how much we can get done in cabin three. The plumbers are supposed to be here tomorrow and I don't want anything in their way to slow them down."

Mack retrieved his tool belt and joined

Dwayne in the cart. He had a lot to think about. Maybe there was some way to show Carly her dad's true character, prove that he hadn't cheated. He had no idea how to go about it. For now, there was only one solution. He'd turn it over to the Lord and ask to be used in the process.

More than anything he wanted to give Carly peace.

Tuesday rolled around faster than Carly expected and she struggled to decide whether to go to the widow's group or not. Deep down she sensed she needed the connection with the other widows, but her head kept telling her that she was fine.

Thelma settled the situation when she announced she was taking the girls for pizza at the Marina Village for supper. With no reasonable excuse to cling to, Carly drove into Hastings and the two-story brick building that housed Nina Johnson Sinclair's office.

The moment she stepped inside, she immediately felt at ease and was glad she'd come. The women all smiled and greeted her. It was like a special club she'd joined. A couple of the ladies were missing and a new one had joined the group—an older woman named Martha who lost her husband in a diving accident a few years ago. She was looking to find courage to move on and try new things, but she was reluctant.

Carly let the conversations swirl around her, gleaning tidbits about widowhood and embracing little kernels of insight the others shared. A sudden need to ask a question surfaced and she spoke up as soon as she had the chance. "I was wondering if any of you have remembered things from your past that weren't quite like you recalled?"

Several ladies nodded, making Carly curious. Martha spoke up. "You get a little distance and perspective on life as you age, and one day you look back and realize that your mom wasn't strict because she didn't like you— she'd been raised in a home without rules and boundaries and she compensated by being overly controlling."

Donna nodded. "That's so true. I remember reading a column in a local paper written by a humorist. She told a story about how each Easter, her mom took a ham, cut it in half and cooked it in two pans. So when the daughter grew up she did the same thing. Until one day she finally asked her mom why she cut the ham in half and used two pans. Her mom shrugged and said it was because she didn't have a pan big enough."

The ladies laughed.

Nina nodded. "Sometimes we go along with things and don't even ask why. We tend to accept instead of searching for the reasons behind things. That's especially true in relationships. Often we look on the surface and come to judgment without taking a closer look. The old adage 'things aren't always what they seem' is true more times than not."

The discussion that followed resonated with Carly on several levels, and she sorted through it in her mind as she drove home.

She pulled the car to a stop in front of the apartment. Was there more to her parents' divorce than what she'd been told? Her mom had suffered greatly from her father's infidelity. But Mack's conviction that her father would never cheat couldn't be ignored. Something in his tone spoke to his deeply held belief that her father was innocent.

There was only one way to find answers. Dig up the truth. The answers had to be here in the Marina community. And of course with her mother. But that wasn't a path she was ready to take yet. Perhaps she should see what she could find out on her own. She wasn't ready for that, either, but she had to know the truth once and for all.

* * *

Mack lifted a wiggly worm from the box and held it up. Lucy reached for it, but Ella drew back.

"Ew!"

Mack grinned. "I thought you girls wanted to learn to fish. First you have to put the fish food on the hook." It had taken longer than he'd expected to arrange the fishing adventure for the girls, but today had been too perfect to let it slip by.

"I'll do it." Lucy took the worm between her fingers. "Will you help, Uncle Mack?"

"Sure." He held the hook and attached the worm. "Okay, now put the line in the water and wait while I get Ella's line ready."

Ella still had her face scrunched up in disgust. "Do I *have* to touch the worm?"

"No. I can put it on for you." She nodded and relaxed her expression. When it was ready, he handed her the cane pole and helped her settle in. He attended to his own pole next. "Okay, now we watch the bobber and when it goes under the water, then we pull up on the fishing pole and we'll catch our fish."

"I'm going to catch a big one."

"Last time Uncle Mack and I fished all I caught was some twigs."

Sandwiched between the two little girls, his spirits began to lift. It was a beautiful day, warm but not too hot. Perfect for sitting on the dock swinging your feet and waiting for the fish to bite. But the best part was simply spending time with his niece and Carly's little girl.

"How long do we have to wait?" Lucy looked up at him with a frown. "Maybe the fish aren't hungry."

Mack smiled at his niece's serious tone.

"Are you sure they like worms, Mr. Mack?" Ella asked.

Lucy glanced up at him. "Maybe we should go out in the boat and fish. Wouldn't that be better, Uncle Mack?"

"Maybe next time. Ella, put your line back in. The fish can't find the worm if it's not in the water."

Mack let the girls' chatter swirl around him. How long had it been since he'd taken a few moments to relax? Since becoming Lucy's guardian his life had grown more hectic. He'd had no idea how much time and thought went into raising a child. And a girl at that. He might have been less stressed if Lucy had been a Luke. But he had to admit he was captivated by her little girl ways and the way she would climb into his lap and make his heart melt like an ice cube on hot concrete.

His admiration for single parents had grown exponentially. Carly was doing a great job with Ella, but he was concerned about her financial burden. No wonder she wanted to sell the lodge. He understood completely, and if he wasn't so emotionally attached to the place he'd go along with her wish to sell out. But his heart was tied up with Longleaf lodge. It was his home in many ways, even more than the one he'd shared with his mother. He also knew how important the business had been to his friend Wade. He'd wanted the legacy for his niece. He couldn't simply let it go without a fight.

"I didn't know we were having a fishing tournament."

Mack turned his head as Carly came toward them along the dock from across the lawn. The sunlight bounced off her silky hair and brightened the brown in her eyes to gold. The simple green sundress she wore fluttered around her calves. She was even more beautiful than he'd remembered. Each time he saw her he was captivated.

"Mommy, I'm fishing. Mr. Mack put the worm on the hook, though. It was too yucky for me."

She stopped beside Ella and sat down on the wooden dock, dangling her feet like the rest of them.

"My dad and I used to fish from this dock a lot."

Lucy grinned. "Next time we're going out in the boat, aren't we?"

Mack glanced at Carly. "If that's okay."

Carly touched the little life jacket her daughter wore. "Thank you for taking precautions."

"I wouldn't let anything happen to either of the girls."

"No, of course not. I should have realized that."

Mack looked past Carly. "You expecting company?"

Carly turned her head. "No."

A balding man in a button-down shirt approached across the grass. "I'm looking for Mrs. Hughes."

Carly quickly got to her feet and greeted the man. "I'm Mrs. Hughes."

"Russell DeLong. We spoke earlier."

Mack watched Carly's shoulders stiffen before she glanced at him and then quickly started toward the house. "Yes. Of course. Why don't we go into the office."

Something in the way she carried herself set off alarms in Mack's head. He ended the fishing as quickly as he could and sent the girls on to Thelma, then went in search of Carly.

He found them in the lodge office, and from the look on her face Carly was liking what the man said. Which meant he wouldn't.

He took a moment to calm his anger and concern, then stepped into the room.

Carly looked up, the blood draining from her face when she saw Mack come into the room. He was the last person she wanted in on this conversation. Before she could speak, he stepped forward and extended his hand. "I don't believe we've met."

"I'm Russell DeLong. I'm very interested in acquiring this property for development."

Mack tossed a hard glare in her direction.

"Mackenzie Bridges. I'm the other heir to the Longleaf Lodge."

Carly's hopes faded. She pressed her lips together.

DeLong glanced between them, obviously confused. "I understood that I was dealing with the owner's daughter."

"And me. We're both listed in the will Mr. Porter left. His daughter inherited the lodge, but I inherited the land. Makes for a sticky situation, don't you think?"

"Indeed it does."

Mack took a seat beside DeLong and crossed his legs, assuming a casual posture. Carly knew him well enough to read below the surface and see that he was covering his irritation with a veneer of friendly interest.

DeLong shifted his attention to Carly but cast a glance at Mack, as well. "I was telling Mrs. Hughes that my partner and I are looking to create a family-oriented resort on this side of the lake. Something that will offer an alternative to the high-priced options of the chain resort."

"Well, that's exactly what we already have here. Longleaf has always appealed to families and those who want a quiet outdoor experience with time to reflect and enjoy their kids."

"Yes, but we'd like to do more than offer a pool and hiking trails."

"Such as?"

Carly cringed at the challenging tone in Mack's voice.

"Well, for starters we'd build a water park with a lazy river feature and wave pool, then we'd triple the number of rooms available at the lodge, as well as increasing the current campsites and RV pads."

"And what are you offering for the property, Mr. DeLong?"

Carly bit her lip. Mack was not going to

be happy. DeLong made his offer and Mack smiled slowly. He stood and held out his hand. "Thank you for coming, Mr. DeLong, but I don't think we're interested at the moment. We appreciate you stopping by."

DeLong stood, looking a bit stunned and confused. Mack deftly steered him toward the door, walking with him to the front porch. Carly lowered her head into her hands, dreading the confrontation to come.

Mack entered the office and closed the door. "What are you doing?"

She set her jaw. "I was trying to sell the estate. The way we agreed."

"Selling is one thing. Giving it away is something else. Why didn't you talk to me first? Why did you go behind my back?"

"I didn't intend to. He called and I told him I'd hear his offer. He saw the listing I had posted online before I took it down. His offer was a solid one."

"No. He was trying to steal the place. Carly, he wants to doze everything and build a whole new complex. There won't be anything left of Longleaf. Is that really what you want?"

"Why are you being so stubborn? We agreed that this was the best plan."

"No. I didn't."

"What do you mean?"

"I only agreed to look for a buyer so you'd stay here. I won't ever agree to sell your dad's business. It wouldn't be right."

"So all that talk about understanding my position, my need for money to pay off doctor bills, that was all a lie?"

"I didn't know about the medical bills at the time. I do understand, but there has to be another solution."

"What? The way things are going we'll never get the lodge open in time to meet the deadline. Nothing is going on schedule."

"Yes, we will. I haven't given up."

"You lied to me, Mack."

"I'd say we're even."

She couldn't argue with that. "I told you it all happened rather quickly. There wasn't time."

"I'm sorry, but I couldn't just let you hand this place over to some stranger. It's your family legacy."

She wanted to deny his words but for some reason she couldn't. Longleaf had been in her family for three generations. Did she have the right to turn her back and walk away? "I understand what you're saying, but look around. We're not making a whole lot of progress here. The young man Thelma hired to run the snack bar can't start for weeks. Not to mention the electricians and plumbers who keep missing their appointments. We're already three weeks into our timeline, and all we have is a few maids and an arrangement with the local bakery. Oh, and thanks to the rain, we haven't even cleared the trails yet."

"But, on the plus side, we have a new roof on a cabin, the canoes are being repaired, and the campsites are all set. I'll get to the trails this week."

"Mack. No matter what you say, I'm not going to change my mind. I don't want to run the lodge. I want my life back in Atlanta. Sorry if you don't believe me, but that's the truth."

"I don't believe you. I remember how much you loved this place. We talked about it all the time. You had ideas for making the place better."

"I was a kid with silly dreams."

"Not silly, Carly. It was a vision for a future." He came closer. "As a matter of fact, I remember you drawing up a plan for adding several attractions to the grounds not too different from what that DeLong guy mentioned."

Carly turned away. She remembered. They'd huddled in one of the pavilions, and she'd drawn out her ideas for making the grounds more exciting. She'd even shared her ideas with her dad and he'd been enthusiastic, as well. He was always looking for ways to improve the campgrounds.

"That was a long time ago. Right now I just want to get through this mess my father left behind."

"Fine. Then I need to get back to work. I'll be at the big cabin if you need me." He turned and strode out.

Carly covered her eyes, trying to sort through the mess. Mack had agreed to sell only as a ploy to gain more time. Hoping she would change her mind. If he was serious about never letting the lodge go, then she had a problem. Now she had to find a way to change *his* mind.

Scooping Spackle onto the trowel, he spread it smoothly along the seams in the drywall, feathering it out across the surface. His emotions still stung from Carly's meeting with the prospective buyer. He'd always thought he and Carly were on the same page when he worked here, but now he found they were not only working against each other, but doing so with animosity. He didn't like fighting with Carly.

A distant roll of thunder broke the silence. There was band of storms heading this way. He welcomed the weather. It suited his dark mood. He'd be trapped in the cabin alone to do his work without interruption. The harder he worked, the easier it was to keep thoughts of Carly at bay.

Once again he sent up a prayer of gratitude for Thelma. With all that was going on, he didn't have to worry about Lucy. He knew she'd be happy as long as she was with her surrogate granny and her friend Ella.

Mack heard the crunch of gravel as a truck pulled up outside. He glanced over his shoulder as Dwayne strode in. He made a quick survey of the space. "Coming along good."

"I guess." He filled his trowel again and spread it over another section of seam. He could sense his friend's concern from across the room.

"Something got your hackles up?"

Mack smeared another trowel of Spackle, fighting the urge to tell the older man to back off. But Dwayne understood Carly better than anyone and it would accomplish nothing by being curt. He set the trowel and tray on the sawhorse and faced his friend. "Carly had a meeting with a potential buyer."

"And she didn't tell you."

The understanding in Dwayne's voice eased Mack's irritation. "No. She went behind my back."

"It's logical, don't you think, considering you're not being honest with her about selling? Maybe it's time to clear the air and let her know your true position."

Mack crossed his arms over his chest. "I did. She didn't take it well."

Dwayne shook his head. "I can talk to her if you think it will help."

"I doubt if she'll listen to anything either of us would say."

"She needs more time."

"Not sure there's enough time in the universe to make her change her mind."

Dwayne patted his back. "Give it a little longer. She has a lot of hurt to dig through."

Mack nodded, returning to his work after Dwayne left. What about his hurt? The hurt Carly had left behind had never gone away. Having her back at the lake had forced him to realize that his love for her had never faded.

Maybe he should get on board with her plan and let the lodge go. He could still provide a good home for Lucy. He had his job with the sheriff's department in Gulfport and he could find them a small house to live in instead of his small apartment. Logically it made sense, but his heart shouted it was wrong.

Carly closed her eyes, replaying the moment Mack had stormed out of her father's office, his shoulders squared, his neck stiff and each step revealing his anger. She'd made a mistake by not telling him about the meeting with De-Long. Foolishly she'd thought the man would make a decent offer, and she and Mack would be happy with a quick settlement. She'd underestimated Mack's affection for the campgrounds. His love for the lodge ran as deep as her father's. She'd have to apologize. Having Mack as an enemy wouldn't help either of them.

She'd been wrong about that day when she had seen Mack and her dad go off together. She was beginning to wonder if she'd been wrong about other things, too. Perhaps Mack had a point. Maybe she should dig a little deeper into the reasons behind her parents' divorce. All she really knew was what her mom had told her. It had been a long time ago and her mom had been married twice since then. Maybe she was ready to open up about the end of her marriage to her father and help her understand.

Plus, there was the slip of the tongue last time they spoke when she had mentioned Richard. Who was Richard?

It took Carly a half hour to gather up the courage to call her mom. Their phone conversations were usually tense and awkward. She'd tried FaceTime with her, but it made her mom self-conscious, and texting was too impersonal.

"Hi, Mom. It's me. How are you?"

"Fine, dear. I can't talk long. Sanford and I are going to a cocktail party with friends. Are you back home now?"

"No, Mom, there's still a lot to do here at the lodge before we can settle the estate."

"It's just like your father to force you to keep that business of his. He was determined to hang on to that money pit."

"He loved it, Mom."

"That's all he loved."

"Is that why you got divorced? Because he ignored you?"

"He cheated. Again and again. I'd had enough."

"Did you catch him?"

"I didn't have to. A woman knows these things. Besides, I saw him talking to that Bonnie person once too often. I knew what was up."

"Bonnie who?"

"I don't want to talk about this with you. It's over and done."

"Mom, who is this Richard you mentioned?"

Her mother inhaled a sharp breath. "Where did you hear that name?"

"You mentioned it to me the last time we talked. You said if Richard had been where he was supposed to be, things would have been different."

"I have no idea what you're talking about. I need to go. I need to get ready for the party. Hurry and finish up down there so you can go home."

Carly made vague promises before hanging up. She was more confused than ever and more determined to find answers. At least now she had a name. Bonnie. The Lake Hope community was small and close-knit. If she could find someone who had been living here around the time of her parents' split, maybe they could fill in some blanks.

A part of her wanted Mack to be right—that her father hadn't been unfaithful. But if that were true, then she'd been horribly unfair to him—and she had a long overdue confrontation with her mother in her future.

Coming home had not only unearthed her long-buried emotions, but now it was uncovering things she wished she didn't know.

The conversation with her mother left her edgy and restless. She sat at her father's large rustic desk, her mind seeing her dad sitting here happily going over every detail of his beloved campgrounds. He used to draw out his ideas on legal paper, things like new trails he wanted to add, a better design for the dock or a special launch pier for the canoes.

One by one she opened the drawers but found only normal business files. Her gaze drifted to the large cabinet in the corner. He'd stored old blueprints there. She sorted through things and found a long roll of paper different from the rest. Spreading it out on the desk, she saw it was a layout of the lodge and the campgrounds, but very different from the way it was right now.

The lodge was bigger, the number of RV pads had been expanded, the camping sites upgraded. Two new playgrounds, a climbing wall and volleyball court were new. A fitness obstacle course had been added, along with a hedge maze and additional cabins. A note about adding a new plot of land was scribbled in the upper right-hand corner.

Her dad had plans to expand and make the Longleaf more appealing to a wider range of families. Yet nothing had been done. Why? He had the money, why didn't he do these things?

She was growing tired of the mounting number of questions and contradictions. Her mom always claimed she was shorted on her child support. If that were true—and he had the money—why didn't he go through with the improvements?

Carly went in search of Dwayne, but he and Thelma had taken the girls to the marina for ice cream. That left Mack. Not her first choice given the recent disagreement, but she needed answers. Now.

Thunder rumbled across the sky as she hurried out to the golf cart. A storm was coming. Perfect. It matched the one brewing inside her. Pressing the accelerator, she steered the small vehicle toward the cabins, keeping the throttle full.

Only when she pulled to a stop at the large cabin did she have second thoughts about confronting Mack again. A flash of lightning spurred her on. She needed to get inside, out of this approaching storm.

And into a storm of a different kind.

Chapter Seven

Mack put the lid on the Spackle can and tapped it tight with a mallet. He heard the golf cart pull up and watched Carly enter the cabin. She was the last person he'd expected to see so soon after their disagreement.

She stopped inside the door and surveyed the area, a large roll of paper held in her hand.

"I thought you'd be further along. What have you been doing all this time? This will never be ready for guests by the deadline."

Mack swallowed the curt remark on his tongue. "Probably not. You seem to forget there are only two of us working on most of these repairs, and the plumber and electrician are trying to work us in around their other jobs as a favor to your dad, but we're not the only place in town needing them."

"How long will those repairs take?"

"Just depends on what else pops up. Unfortunately, we seem to find new issues every day. I think your dad was holding a lot of things together with a hope and a prayer."

Carly exhaled an exasperated huff. "I can't believe this. We're running out of time."

Mack set his jaw. "No one's giving up yet, Carly. What have you got there?"

"I found this in Dad's office." She spread it out on the counter. "They're plans for a huge expansion." Mack leaned over her shoulder, keenly aware of how her nearness always caused a skip in his pulse. A clap of thunder shook the cabin, causing Carly to jump back against him.

"Still afraid of storms?"

"Of course not. It was just unexpected, that's all." She glanced over her shoulder to the open door as the sky opened up and a curtain of rain poured down. "We'll never get done if the rain keeps coming."

"I checked the radar. It's a narrow band. Won't last long. Unfortunately the forecast calls for showers nearly every day for the next week or so." He tapped the drawing with his fingertips, pulling her attention back to the plans. She glanced at him briefly, then down at the drawing.

"These are all the things we used to talk

about a long time ago. Do you know anything about this?"

"No. I never saw it." He looked at the date on the designs. "This was drawn up after I went off to Mississippi College in Jackson. This would have been the summer you came back."

"Why didn't he follow through on this? It even looks like he was thinking of buying more land to expand the campgrounds. We never talked about that."

"Wade was always looking for ways to make Longleaf better and more appealing to guests."

"I know, so why didn't he follow through?"

Mack had a pretty good idea, but he hesitated to share it.

Carly wasn't fooled. "What? What aren't you telling me?"

"If I had to guess, I'd say he gave up on the idea after you left that summer after the divorce."

"What does that have to do with anything?"

He leaned back against the counter and crossed his arms over his chest. "He looked forward to you coming home that summer. That's all he talked about. He wanted to celebrate your seventeenth birthday, but you only stayed a week, then ran away."

She set her jaw, brown eyes flashing. "I didn't run away. Why does everyone think that?"

"Because that's exactly what it looked like. To everyone. After you left he was different. I think he was hoping you'd be with him all summer and that you could repair your relationship, but you didn't give it a chance. It was as if you couldn't stand to be around him. I think it broke his spirit. He was different after that." He searched her gaze for some flicker of regret, but she looked away quickly. "Why *did* you leave so suddenly?"

Carly blanched. "I had my reasons."

"You didn't even say goodbye. To me or your dad or the Thompsons."

Carly rolled up the designs. "I had to get back to my mom. She needed me."

"Your dad needed you, too."

She whirled around and pinned him with a glare. "He had you. I'm sure that was more than enough." She strode to the door, then stopped as another roll of thunder boomed.

Mack stepped up behind her, watching the rain pour off the roof. Soon it eased up, signaling the end of the storm and triggering a memory.

"Do you remember that day we were closing the cabins for the season and a storm blew in, and we ducked in here to get out of the rain?"

Carly nodded and smiled, warmed by the memory. "We sat on the porch for an hour waiting for it to stop. That's the first time I heard you talk about being a lawyer. I was so proud of you."

"And you were going to work alongside your dad at the lodge."

"That was a long time ago. I didn't know any better." She looked over her shoulder at him and their gazes met and held.

He told himself to look away, but he'd always been drawn by her lovely eyes. He was so close to her it would only take a shift of his arm to pull her around into his arms. Her gaze softened, and her lips parted slightly in a silent invitation. Dare he risk the consequences?

Distant thunder broke the spell and Carly quickly darted away, slid into the golf cart and drove off, leaving him with the same melancholy feeling he'd experienced years ago.

He was such a fool.

Carly parked her car and slipped her phone into her purse. Ashley's phone call had been a welcome interruption after Carly's visit to the cabin. Her pulse still raced when she thought about the moment when she'd looked into Mack's eyes and knew he wanted to kiss her. The memory of the kiss they'd shared long ago had made her want to repeat the experience. Thankfully, they'd both come to their senses and she'd hurried off. No. Run off. Her attraction to Mack was starting to grow, and she wasn't sure how she felt about it. She was just as confused about her feelings for him today as she had been that summer. The difference was she'd been a dreamy-eyed teen with a crush on the older boy. She was a woman now, and she understood attraction and chemistry between a man and a woman, and she knew it wasn't enough to take seriously. Thankfully, a call from her old friend requesting a meeting was exactly what she needed to shove dangerous memories of Mack from her mind.

Ashley waved and joined Carly at the charming bistro table on the deck outside the Perked Up coffee shop at the Marina Village. She'd been anxious to discuss something, and Carly hoped Ashley might be able to help her track down the woman named Bonnie.

"Thanks for coming, Carly."

"You sounded serious. Is everything okay?"

"Yes, I just wanted to ask you a question, well, more like ask for your help." She took a deep breath. "I've been visiting your website about the lodge and following you on social media. And I'm so impressed. Anyone who visits your sites and sees those pictures you're posting will be pounding on your door for reservations."

"I have to admit we've been receiving inquiries. I just wish I could give them a solid date for the opening. You know we have a deadline and if we don't meet it, we could lose everything."

"I know. But I don't see that happening. You have a real gift for marketing. I've been over every inch of the campgrounds with you growing up, but I'm seeing it in a whole new light through that website and your stunning pictures."

"That's encouraging. Thanks. I have to admit taking pictures of the campgrounds has reminded me how beautiful Longleaf is and why people enjoy coming here."

"So here's my question. Would you be willing to work your magic for me and the store? I'm really bad with social media. I've tried to get the hang of that stuff, but I'm always too busy with work and taking care of the kids. My eight-year-old knows more about it than I do. I just thought… If I could hire you to promote my business, it would free me up to concentrate on the actual work."

Carly mulled over the idea. "I suppose I could do that. Once I had things set up, it wouldn't take any longer to broadcast your information than it does for the lodge. And I'm already doing postings for my job back in Atlanta."

"Thank you. That would be such a blessing. I'm just not very savvy about what to do to draw people in. Business in the village is growing, but there are still so many who don't know we're here. Publicity would benefit all of us."

Carly laid out a quick plan for Ashley, promising to return and take pictures before heading home. She hadn't planned on turning her new virtual-assistant position into a real job, but she was beginning to wonder if it might not be a way to earn extra income. It was definitely worth considering.

Carly drove home from the Marina Village with a lightness in her heart that had been absent for a long time. Ashley's request had fueled an idea that was quickly taking root. Maybe she could start her own business, a virtual-assistant service, doing the social media tasks that so many business owners found frustrating or overwhelming. It was working well for her boss, Jessie, at the shop and it was gaining momentum for the lodge. Adding the marina store to the list would be easy. If it went well, she might be able to add more village stores.

Thelma was sitting on the back deck watching the girls play when Carly came home. They had the two little dogs, Poppy and Petunia, in a small baby carriage and were pushing them around the yard.

"Looks like they're having fun. Is that my old doll carriage?"

"It is. I found it in the storage room under the lodge. There are a bunch of your old toys in there."

"Really? I would have thought Dad would have gotten rid of that stuff a long time ago."

"They belonged to you. He would never dream of parting with them."

Carly's heart pinched. She couldn't keep pretending that her dad didn't care. There was too much evidence stacking up to prove otherwise.

"Did you have a nice visit with your friend?"

"I did." She took a seat in the cushioned chair beside Thelma. "In fact, she wants to hire me to handle her social media."

"Like you're doing here?"

"Yes. I'm beginning to think it might be a viable business for me. I could work from the lodge and spend more time with Ella. If it goes well with Ashley, then I might be able to expand to the other businesses in the Marina Village."

Thelma studied her. "Are you thinking about staying here permanently, then?"

Carly jerked her head toward the woman. "What? No. Why?"

"You said you could work from here, at the lodge."

Carly realized her mistake. "It was a slip of the tongue."

"Of course. Well, Dwayne and Mack want to have a meeting at supper to see where we are on the repair list. I'm fixing pork chops tonight. Your favorite."

Carly smiled. "Dad and I loved your cooking. Why don't I help you?"

"I'd like that. I always enjoyed it when you helped in the kitchen."

Carly's anxiety about the meeting rose steadily as the afternoon wore on, despite her playing with the girls and the puppies on the lawn and starting a plan for Ashley's business. However, it looked to her like little progress was being made toward opening the lodge. She prayed the update tonight would prove her wrong. Helping Thelma prepare the meal kept her mind off it all. The girls had been seated at the counter and were shredding the lettuce for a salad when Dwayne and Mack strolled in. Carly avoided making eye contact with Mack, afraid her confusion over their almost kiss would show on her face.

They settled at the table. Dwayne said grace and the food was passed around. It smelled delicious, but Carly feared she wouldn't taste a bite of it. Thankfully, the conversation centered on mundane things. The girls talked about the baby carriage they'd played with and the promise of more old toys to enjoy from the storage room. Carly shared Ashley's request for social media assistance. As usual the girls finished their meal first and asked to be excused to watch a video. With them out of the room, Dwayne rested his elbows on the table and clasped his hands.

Carly held her breath braced for bad news. The look in Mack's eyes reinforced her concern.

She wasn't going to like what she was about to hear.

Mack toyed with his fork. He'd half expected Carly to miss this meeting with the Thompsons. Dealing with the to-do list caused her anxiety. He could tell by her posture that she was tense and edgy about the updates. She wanted everything done instantly, and he knew that was not how anything worked in this life. There was a lot to do and everything had to go according to plan and in a certain order. He'd flipped enough houses to know that rarely happened. But he would do his best. For all their sakes.

Carly didn't wait for them to start. "Where

do we stand on getting this place open? I was by the big cabin today and it didn't look like much progress had been made. I'm getting worried. Will the cabins be open soon? I'm already getting requests for registrations."

Dwayne took a sip of his sweet tea. "That cabin probably won't be ready, but the others should be. The electricians should be here tomorrow and the plumbers the day after. I've looked at the pipes in cabin number one and it might be a bigger job than we thought. They probably will have to replace a large section of the drainage run. Then we'll still have to wait for the inspections before we can allow guests on the property."

"How long will that take? We're running out of time."

Mack tapped his electronic tablet and scanned the list. "We've made considerable progress. Cabin two's roof is done and the canoes will be returned tomorrow. The AC units in the lodge are working and I patched the holes in the walls. As you saw, the big cabin still needs painting, new floors and new furniture. Dwayne's right. I don't think it'll be ready in time."

"And the trails?"

"We haven't been able to clear them because of the frequent rain."

Carly pressed her lips together. "What does that leave?"

Thelma sighed. "I don't have good news on my end I'm afraid. The repairs to the rooms are completed, but it's taking longer than I anticipated to get our supplies ordered and delivered. The lodge kitchen will be steam cleaned on Friday, but then I don't know how long it'll take to get the health department to come and inspect it." She glanced at the list on her notepad. "I felt sure I could rehire most of our former employees, but it's been too long. They had to move on to other jobs. I did manage to get Blanche Messier back to manage the rooms and the maids. She'll be able to handle all those preparations. I've also found a young college student to run the snack bar at the pool. He worked fast food last year so he knows what's expected, though he can't start work for a few weeks."

Mack knew Thelma well enough to sense there was more. "What else?"

"Our former chef has taken a job in Mobile. Finding another one will take a while. We might be able to manage with a cook if we offered a buffet for each meal, but we'd still have to hire waiters and I'm having trouble finding suitable people."

Carly spoke up. "What if we didn't open the

kitchen? What if we offered a simple continental breakfast only? With the snack bar at the pool open during the day, the guests can get hot dogs, burgers and nachos there. Of course the campers like grilling their own food anyhow. And there are several restaurants at the new Marina Village for guests to go to for dinner. And the new hotel, of course."

Thelma nodded. "That could work. The goal is to be open for business, but we don't have to have all the amenities available, do we?"

Mack rubbed his jaw. "I don't think so, but I'll check with the attorney. Time's running out and there's still a lot to do."

"Mack and I will have our repairs done in time. It's all a matter of the subcontractors and how quickly they can make their repairs." Dwayne shrugged. "Though I have been leaning on them to give us a break since it's for Wade. They're more than willing, but they still have to finish other jobs first."

"Then we'll pray that they work swiftly." Thelma patted her husband's arm.

Carly pushed back from the table and stood. "In the meantime I'm going to focus on the website for the lodge and getting the word out. We've got to start getting people interested in staying here."

Mack's ringtone sounded and he glanced

at the screen, then quickly moved off. Carly watched his expression shift from irritation to concern to stern resolve. His jaw flexed, sending a twinge of concern along her nerves. "Is everything all right?"

Mack took a long moment to reply. "I've been called into work."

"Work? I don't understand."

"The sheriff's department is organizing a manhunt for three escaped prisoners and they need all hands on deck."

A cold chill raced through her system. She'd never thought much about Mack's real line of work. In her mind he was always the guy who worked at the lodge. "But you don't work for the sheriff's department. Why are they calling you?"

"I'm assigned to them on a temporary basis. It's the only way I could get the time to stay here at the lodge."

"How long will you be gone?"

"As long as they need me. Could be a few days or weeks."

"But you're needed here. Can't you explain that to them?"

"And what about the people in danger from the escaped prisoners?"

Carly's cheeks turned bright red. "Sorry."

Dwayne spoke up. "Mack's absence might

slow things a bit, but it's time for the subcontractors to take over. The three of us can handle the rest."

"It'll be all right, Carly." He held her gaze a moment. "I need to talk to Thelma about Lucy."

"Mack, she can stay with us while you're gone. I know Ella would love to have her."

"Thanks. I'll let you and Thelma work that out. I'm going to get my gear, then I'll say goodbye to Lucy."

Carly watched him walk out, felt a strange knot forming in her center. She knew Mack was a deputy, but it hadn't really registered until this moment. She couldn't help but wonder what kind of danger he would be in.

Fear clamped onto her heart like a cold vise.

Nothing could happen to Mack.

She couldn't handle it.

Mack climbed out of his SUV, adjusting his utility belt as he walked up to the front door of the lodge. It felt good to be back at work. He loved law enforcement, but he loved working at the lodge, too. Each gave him a different kind of satisfaction. He had to admit, though, now that Lucy was part of his life, working as a deputy put him too much in harm's way. He was all his niece had. Could he risk his life to provide for her?

He stepped inside the lodge and Lucy bounded toward him. "Uncle Mack, I heard your car. Why are you going away?"

"I have to catch some bad guys."

"Oh. Like you did back home?"

"Yes. You're going to stay here with Thelma."

"And Ella and her mom. We're going to take turns sleeping. One night at Ella's house, and one night at Miss Thelma's."

"That sounds like fun."

She hugged his neck. "Will you be gone long?"

"I don't know, sweet pea. I hope not. I'll miss you."

Mack saw Carly enter the lobby and come toward him. "She'll be fine, Mack. I promise. We'll take good care of her."

"I'm not worried. Besides, I have someone special to come home to." He looked into Carly's eyes and saw questions forming. He grinned, then placed a kiss on Lucy's cheek before setting her down. "My number one girl." She waved and hurried off to find Ella.

Carly stood silent and stiff in front of him. "Something wrong?" he asked.

"I just never saw you in uniform before." She swallowed. "You look good." She reached out and lightly touched his shirt. "The blue matches the color of your eyes." She jerked back her hand and cleared her throat. "You look very authoritative."

He grinned. "Thanks, I think. I've been told women like a man in uniform."

"I think it's the sense of protection and security it implies."

He had the strangest feeling they were talking about something entirely different, but that wasn't possible. Was it? The look in her eyes said she was attracted. If wearing his uniform could solicit that kind of response from Carly, then he'd wear it every day.

He cleared his throat. "That's our creed. To protect and serve. Though actually that refers to protecting and serving the law, not the individual." He saw her gaze shift. He should have quit while he was ahead.

"I'd better hit the road. I'll have my phone with me if something comes up. If Lucy needs me, don't hesitate to call." He held her gaze again, this time seeing concern with a hint of affection—at least, that was what he hoped it was.

He turned to go but she hurried after him, taking his arm to pull him around.

"Mack, please be careful. I— We wouldn't want anything to happen to you." She stood on tiptoe and placed a kiss on his cheek, enveloping him in the heady scent of spring flowers, sending his heart thumping.

"So, you're worried about me?"

"No. Yes, I mean. We're friends and you're going into a dangerous situation."

He grinned and touched her chin lightly with his fingertips. "Yes, we are."

He turned and walked out, climbing into his vehicle and replaying Carly's actions again in his mind. His heart was light knowing that she cared about him—even if it was only because he was a cop. But it gave him hope that maybe, in time, she could look at him differently, as someone more than the obstacle between her and the money she needed. The man trying to force her to relive her youth.

An hour later Mack met up with Sheriff Walker Jones and the other officers at the Lenard County headquarters in Hastings and got his assignment. He and two other deputies would set up a command post near the rural town of Trent in the southeast quadrant of the county, where the convicts were suspected of going.

He sent up a prayer for a quick recovery of the escapees and safety for the men involved in the search. He'd been in this situation before and it hadn't ended well. For the first time in years he seriously questioned his line of work. He used to only have himself to think about; now he had Lucy, and maybe Carly and Ella.

He shelved those thoughts and focused on the job ahead. It wasn't a good idea to go off on a manhunt with personal concerns clouding his mind.

However, it might take more effort than normal, given that soft look in Carly's gaze.

Chapter Eight

Carly took a sip of her sweet tea while watching the girls on the playground equipment at the edge of the Fishing Hole Restaurant at the Marina Village. The area was designed to look like a Gulf Coast beach complete with white-sugar sand. She'd decided to treat the girls to pizza to get them out of the lodge. Lucy had gotten upset because, with Mack away on duty, her mom couldn't call. Carly hoped pizza and a little shopping would take her mind off her disappointment. The girls had picked out matching purple sundresses and flip-flops with big lavender flowers on the toes. They wanted to match like twins.

Too bad she couldn't distract her own thoughts as easily. Mack had been gone nearly a week. She knew he couldn't call and chat, but she'd hoped he'd text her to let her know he was all right. Her imagination had been working overtime conjuring up dangerous scenarios he might be caught up in.

Seeing him in his uniform with the gun on his hip had hit hard. The realization of his job, of what he risked day to day, had settled like a stone in her center. The thought of something happening to him had forced her real feelings to the surface. She still cared for Mack Bridges and in more than a friendly way.

"Carly. I thought that was you." Ashley sat down beside her, nudging her shoulder. "Taking a break from the lodge?"

"Just a little break for the girls."

"Which one is yours?"

She pointed to the pair who were now sharing a child-sized hammock between two fake palm trees. "The dark-haired one. The blonde is Mack's niece, Lucy."

"I heard about his sister. It's so sad. Mack has had a lot to overcome in his life."

"Haven't we all?"

Ashley squeezed her hand. "Yes, we have."

Carly was immediately contrite. Her friend knew only too well the struggles of losing a husband. "I'm sorry. I'm just a little out of sorts today."

"Hang in there. Only a few more days until the widow's group. I always feel better after I've met with the ladies. They keep me grounded and help scatter all the gloomy pictures I tend to dwell on."

"I know what you mean." A cloud of gloom had been hovering over her since Mack had left. Between the worry over his safety and the concern about the repairs getting done, she was having trouble concentrating.

"If I'd known you were going to be here, we could have eaten together and let the girls meet my crew."

"That sounds good. Let's do that soon. I know Lucy and Ella would love to make new friends."

Ashley studied her closely. "Anything else on your mind? I can tell you're worried. You get that little crease in your forehead."

She'd forgotten how close she and Ashley had once been. "I'm worried about Mack."

"Why? He looked like his usual handsome self when I saw him last week." She grinned.

"He's been called up to help the sheriff's department search for those prisoners who escaped."

"Oh, wow. I didn't realize he was a cop."

"He was going to be a lawyer, but he liked the hands-on appeal of helping people."

"Sounds like Mack. I've been watching the

evening news reports, and it doesn't sound like they've found them yet."

Carly kept her gaze on her glass. "We've been friends for a long time. I can't help but care."

Ashley patted her knee and stood. "Now all you have to do is figure out how *much* you care."

She shook her head. "Not that much. Don't go spinning romantic fantasies, Ash."

Standing, Carly called to the girls. "Call me and we'll set up a lunch date. I'm anxious to meet your children."

"Will do. In the meantime I'll keep Mack in my prayers. And you, too."

Carly waved as her friend moved off, then walked the girls to the car and headed back to the lodge. Ashley's comment replayed in her mind like a video loop. How much *did* she care for Mack? She had to admit that being around him had sent her senses racing and her thoughts headed down romantic paths she hadn't traveled for a long time. After Troy's death she never expected to have feelings for another man. Their marriage, though short, had been filled with happiness and content-ment. Even when Ella had been diagnosed with her heart condition, they had taken comfort and strength from each other. Troy had been her rock.

But she couldn't deny that her feelings for Mack were growing stronger every day. She just had no idea what she was going to do about it.

Mack moved off to the side of the building in the middle of the staging area in Trent and pulled out his phone. This was the first chance he'd had to check in with Carly and Lucy since he'd left the lodge. Thankfully, he'd been so busy during the day and exhausted at night that he fell into bed with little time to think about his family. But there were moments when the ache of missing them would seize hold, and it took all his power of concentration to keep his mind on his job. He'd prayed the convicts would be captured soon, but so far they were leading the posse on a merry chase. They knew the area and were able to evade capture. Mack was beginning to fear they might not ever be caught.

Carly's phone rang several times before she answered, and the sound of her voice brought an instant smile to his face and forced him to realize how much he missed her. Especially satisfying was the note of joy in her tone. "How are things going back there?"

"Mack, it's so good to hear from you. Are you all right? Will you be home soon? Lucy asks about you every day. Ella, too."

He chuckled. "Whoa. One question at a time. I'm fine. Don't know how much longer, and I miss Lucy, too. I miss all of you." Carly's silence made him wonder if she missed him. He hoped so. "How are things going on your end? Sorry I had to bail on you."

"We're doing all right. I took the girls down the trails and they helped me clear the debris. They seemed to enjoy helping."

"That's good to hear. Did the subcontractors show up?"

"Yes, but they seem to be taking their sweet time with the work. Dwayne assures me they are on schedule, but I don't know."

"Don't worry, Carly. Dwayne will keep their feet to the fire." Mack heard the sheriff call out. "I need to go, but I wanted to let you know I'm being assigned to the northeast corner of the county. They think the prisoners are holed up in an abandoned farm up there. I won't have good cell coverage, so it might be a few days before I can get in touch."

"I understand. Be careful."

"I always am. Is Lucy there? I'd like to say hello to her before I have to hang up." The sound of his niece's sweet little voice warmed his heart even as her pleas to come home wrapped it in a sad ache. He prayed the convicts would be captured soon so he could get back to those he loved. And once back at the lodge he would have to do some soul-searching to see where his life would go from here.

He had never anticipated that Wade's death would set in motion a series of events that might change his life forever.

Slipping his phone into his pocket, he joined the other deputies and closed off his mind to the thoughts of home and family and focused on the job at hand. Distraction could mean death.

Carly gripped her phone tightly, every nerve on alert. Ashley had called, announcing she had important information.

"Remember the other day when you asked me if I knew anyone named Bonnie? I asked around, and apparently there was a woman who lived here and worked part-time at the old marine store."

"Do you know her last name?"

"No, but they said she now works in the office for the developer. It's on the far end of the village. It might not be her, but it's a place to start. She'd remember lots of people from back then."

"Thanks. I'll go see her."

"Carly, don't jump to conclusions, okay? All you have to go on is a name your mom threw out."

"She wouldn't forget something like that."

"You said yourself she didn't always remember things correctly."

"I know. I'll be diplomatic. I promise."

Carly thanked her friend, then ended the call and checked her watch. She had plenty of time to go to the marina and track down this woman while Thelma had the girls at her house. After retrieving the earring from her room, she drove to the marina. Her nerves were on edge. Finally she might have some answers about what really happened with her mother and father.

The village management offices were housed in a simple one-story building at the back of the shopping center. The facade blended in with the rest of the exteriors and no one would know it was there if you weren't looking for it. The inside was quiet and tastefully decorated in shades of gray and cream. A young woman seated at a sleek reception desk glanced up as she entered.

"May I help you?"

"I hope so. I'm looking for a woman named Bonnie. I'm sorry I don't know her last name, but she's worked at the marina for a long time.

I grew up here and I… I'm back in town and thought I'd look her up."

"Oh. Well, I don't know anyone by that name. The only people here are Mr. Garner, the manager, his assistant, Peter, and Miss B. She does the books."

"What does the *B* stand for?"

The woman blinked in surprise. "Oh, I'm not sure. Let me go find out."

She returned quickly with a bright smile. "Guess what? Turns out Miss B is your Bonnie. Follow me and I'll show you to her office."

"Miss B. This lady is here to see you."

The woman stood and Carly was forced to adjust her preconceived image. Bonnie was around her dad's age, with white hair, a friendly face and plump figure that made one think of a sweet grandma. "I'm Bonnie Hudson. Can I help you?"

Just because she looked like a sweet grandma now didn't mean she wasn't attractive years ago. A nervous knot formed in Carly's stomach. This wasn't going to be as easy as she'd expected.

Her fingers closed around the earring, squeezing it so tightly the edge dug into her skin. She had to know the truth. "My name is Carly Porter. Wade Porter was my father."

Her face broke into a wide smile. "Wade's

little girl. Oh, my. You've grown into a beautiful young woman. He was so proud of you. He talked about you all the time."

The cheery response caught her off guard. "You saw a lot of him?"

"I did. He came into the store all the time. I was so sad to hear of his death."

She couldn't make nice any longer. "I have something that belongs to you."

"Me?"

Carly placed the earring on the desk, watching for Bonnie's reaction.

"Oh, my goodness. Where did you find this? I lost it years ago."

Carly set her jaw. "In my father's truck where you left it."

Bonnie frowned. "What exactly are you implying?"

"My mother told me about my father's affairs."

Bonnie's expression softened with sympathy. "I see. Sit down. Perhaps we need to have a talk."

Carly hesitated but finally sat down.

"I never had an affair with your father, or anyone. I'm happily married and have been for forty years."

Bonnie held up the earring. "I was only in your father's vehicle one time. There was a chamber of commerce meeting that night. My husband had just had knee surgery and he couldn't drive me. Wade offered to give me a lift, which I accepted because those things usually ran late. We drove to the meeting and he drove me home." She fingered the jewelry. "I have a habit of taking these off because they pinch after a while. That's probably when I dropped it."

Carly wanted to believe her, but she couldn't get her mother's accusations out of her mind. Bonnie continued before she could speak.

"Your father was a wonderful man and he loved your mother very much, even during their hard times. I think maybe you should talk with your mother and ask her to clear things up for you. It was a long time ago and, sometimes, things get distorted over the years."

Carly felt like the wind had been taken out of her sails. Why would her mother name this woman as someone her father cheated with if he hadn't? Of course Bonnie could be lying, but something deep inside told her she wasn't. She stood. "Thank you for seeing me. I'm so sorry if I've upset you. It's just that my mother was so certain you were... I mean... Please accept my apologies."

"Don't give it another thought, Carly. I'm sorry you've been troubled by this for so long."

Carly gave an apologetic smile, then reached for the door. "Oh, one more thing. Do you know anyone named Richard who would have been living here about the time my parents split up?"

Bonnie blanched and laid a hand at her throat. "Oh, dear. Where did you hear about him?"

"My mother mentioned him, but then she quickly denied knowing him."

"I don't wonder. Richard is my half brother. He was living with us back then for a time. He's a lazy, womanizing moocher who never did an honest day's work in his life."

"Where is he now?"

"I haven't the faintest idea. But if your mother was involved with him, then she has my sympathy."

"Why?"

"That's something else you need to talk to her about."

Carly thanked the woman again and left, her mind a whirlwind of questions and doubts. Why would her mother lie about her father having an affair with Bonnie, and what had gone on between her mother and Richard?

By the time she arrived home, she wanted to cry. In the kitchen she sought out Thelma for some sound advice.

"My goodness, what happened? You look so upset."

Carly took a seat on the stool. "I just met with a woman my mom told me had an affair with my dad."

"Really? Who?"

"Bonnie Hudson."

Thelma kept her gaze on the brownie batter she was mixing. "What did she have to say?"

"She denied it. And I believe her. I just don't understand why Mom would say that if it wasn't true."

"I'm sure I couldn't say."

Thelma was avoiding her. "What about a man named Richard? Do you know anything about him and my mother being involved?"

Thelma stopped stirring and stood still for a long moment before coming around the counter and joining Carly. "Richard was the man your mother was seeing. He was a charmer and he promised her all the things she wanted. She left to meet him at the airport. They were going to run away together. But he never showed up. She waited for days, but he never came back."

Carly's heart pinched. She could only imagine the humiliation. Yet she didn't understand how her mom could simply walk away from her and her dad. "That was the week she was gone. She was supposed to be visiting a friend."

Thelma nodded. "When she came back, she was so angry and hurt and humiliated. She lit into your dad something fierce, accusing him of all kinds of things. Then a few days later she took you and left."

"Why would she do that?"

"I think she was embarrassed to be jilted by a lothario. It was easier to blame her husband for everything. If she accused him of unfaithfulness, then she wouldn't have to face her own poor behavior and judgment."

Tears formed in Carly's eyes. "Why would she let me think that about my dad? She knew how much I loved him."

"Exactly. She knew. How else could she get you to leave him?"

"Why didn't you tell me about this?"

"I tried, but at the time you weren't willing to listen to anyone. You were so angry and so distraught."

It was true. Carly hadn't been in the mood to listen to anyone at that time. "What about that next summer when I came back to visit?"

"I didn't have a chance. You were here a week and then you ran off. You were still pretty upset—with everyone." Thelma opened her arms and embraced her. "I'm so sorry. I should have tried harder. Nothing was the same after you left that last time. It took your father a long time to recover. It's like the heart of him had been ripped out."

Carly clung to the older woman. For the first time in years she felt a strange sense of peace. The truth was emerging. While it wasn't what she'd expected, she knew it was true. It explained so many things.

She wiped her eyes. "Thank you for telling me all this. I think I have a lot of soul-searching to do. Where are the girls?"

"Outside. Where else? I'll look after them. Go take some quiet time."

Carly returned to the apartment, stopping at the large window with a view of the lake. She'd gone in search of the truth, but it was more upsetting than she'd imagined. How did she reconcile what she'd learned with what she'd long believed? A headache formed, and she went upstairs and stretched out on the bed. She wished her dad was here. He'd never lied to her or deceived her. Why had she been so quick to believe the worst about him?

Closing her eyes, she drifted into a troubled sleep. When she awoke she saw that she'd nearly slept through supper and left the care of Lucy and Ella all to Thelma.

She'd spent enough time feeling sorry for herself. It was time to focus on the present. The past couldn't be changed, but she could shape a better future by getting the lodge open and up for sale.

It was the only logical solution.

Mack took up a position behind a tree, gun drawn, his gaze focused on the small clapboard house up ahead. The escaped prisoners had been tracked here after one of them had been injured. A blood trail had been found at the foot of a ravine. Now the deputies had them surrounded, but word had come down that they had amassed a small arsenal of weapons during their flight.

Instructions from the sheriff came through his headset, and Mack acknowledged the command, then motioned his men into position. Every muscle in his body tensed, his mind trained on the task ahead. As he waited for the order to move, a flash of color on the ground caught his eye. A small piece of blue fabric with little yellow flowers was trampled among the leaves and dirt. The colors reminded him of a dress Lucy had picked out. She'd fallen in love with it and given the most pitiful look, begging him to buy it.

He glanced up, his muscles tensing as he

waited. He shouldn't be thinking of Lucy or anything other than what he was going into, but his heart had other ideas. Suddenly being on this manhunt was the last place he wanted to be. The adrenaline rush that usually fueled him at times like these was missing. His throat suddenly tightened and his lungs froze. What if something happened to him? Who would care for Lucy? He should have made arrangements for her. How had he not realized that his job would put her at risk?

"Execute. Execute."

Caught off guard, it took him a second to react. The men advanced on the old house. Shots rang out. Mack returned fire. He moved by instinct and habit, mounting the porch with one leap. A barrage of gunfire erupted. A bullet zinged past his ear. He aimed and fired only to feel something hot against his shoulder.

Gritting his teeth, he charged forward into the chaos.

Carly strolled into the kitchen, engulfed in the tantalizing aroma of chicken and vegetables. "I'm so sorry. I should have been here to help with the meal."

"Nonsense. I have it all under control."

Dwayne set the plates on the table. "Did

you ladies know there's a tropical storm in the Gulf? Looks like it's going to grow into a hurricane pretty quick."

Thelma handed her husband the napkins. "But it's only the first of June. The hurricane season has just started. We don't usually get hurricanes so early."

"No, but it's not unheard-of. Remember last year?" He looked past Carly to the TV in the corner of the kitchen. He stood and hurried toward it, a deep frown on his face.

Carly glanced at the screen and saw a sheriff's deputy being interviewed. The crawl below reported that several officers had been shot during the apprehension of the escaped prisoners. One had died and another was in critical condition. Several were suffering from minor injuries. The officer's names were being withheld pending notification of next of kin.

Carly's blood turned to ice. Her heart refused to beat for a moment, then lodged like a stone in her throat. Mack. Had he been killed? Or shot? He had no next of kin except for his sister. Who would they notify?

Dwayne slipped an arm around her shoulders. "Don't get too upset. We're listed as Mack's emergency contacts and no one has called us. We'll believe the best until we hear differently."

She didn't realize she was shaking until Dwayne eased her onto a stool and she glanced at her hands. She looked at the TV again, trying to control her rapid breathing. "Try another station, maybe there's more news."

Dwayne flipped through the channels, but none of the local networks had anything more to add. For the time being they could only wait. And worry.

She stood, her knees barely holding up her weight. She moved around in a fog, her mind unable to focus on one coherent thought. Blood pounded in her ears, and her heart beat painfully behind her ribs.

Thelma wrapped an arm around her shoulder. "Why don't you go lie down for a while? I'll take the girls up to our place and keep them busy. Dwayne will see what he can find out."

The silence in her living room offered only a brief respite from the shock. Then, like giant waves on the beach, the fear would crash over her again. She curled up in the corner of the sofa, hugging a pillow to her chest. She wanted to cry, but the tears refused to come. The thought of Mack dead, or fighting for his life in the hospital, was too horrible to contemplate. Nothing could happen to him. He was too strong. Too invincible.

He was too important to her. More important than she'd been willing to acknowledge. She'd been ignoring her feelings for Mack from the moment she'd seen him in the lawyer's office. Each encounter had cracked open the sealed compartment of her heart, and the harder she pushed to keep it closed, the harder it had become.

Her gaze drifted to the window and the glimpse of the shimmering lake beyond. She couldn't afford to fall for Mack again. They didn't want the same things. He was the opposition. He wanted to keep the lodge; she wanted out.

A sharp twinge of guilt danced along her nerves. It was time to face a few facts. She was afraid to look too closely at her feelings for Mack because that made her compare them to her love for Troy. And lately she'd been realizing that as much as she loved Troy, he never made her feel the way Mack did. What scared her most was that the two had nothing in common. Was it possible that her love for Troy wasn't the same as her feelings for Mack? What did that say about her?

The disturbing thoughts clogged her throat

and sent her heart into a tight knot. She grabbed the remote and turned on the TV, scanning the channels, but nothing new about the officers was being reported.

The apartment started to close in on her, making it hard to breath. She stood and went to her laptop and did a quick search but found nothing there, either, which only added to her anxiety.

Unable to sit still, she strolled out onto the lawn, seeking comfort in her favorite place, the yard swing at the edge of the water. But this time, the rhythmic sway of the swing and the gentle ripples on the water didn't ease her fears.

She gave in to the horrible truth. What would she do without Mack? He'd been part of her world since she was twelve years old. She'd had a crush on him, even fancied herself in love with him when she was seventeen. Most of her past memories included him one way or another.

What would little Lucy do without him? And Dwayne and Thelma. Mack was the son they never had.

How would any of them go on without him? *Please, Lord, bring him home safe.*

Her text tone sounded and she quickly dug

her phone from her pocket. Her heart raced when she saw it was a text from Dwayne.

Mack is fine. He'll be home tomorrow.

Tension drained from her body like a flood, leaving her weak and light-headed. She sent up thankful prayers as the tears finally began to fall. The thought of seeing him for herself, knowing firsthand that he was safe and whole, made her realize how much he meant to her. And that was something she couldn't let him see. She had to get control of her emotions before he returned tomorrow. She wasn't about to make a fool of herself by revealing her crush, which was all it was. It couldn't be anything else but a rebirth of her childhood feelings from long ago.

There was nothing else at work, because she'd already had the love of her life and she'd married him. There could never be another man like Troy.

She stood and headed back to the lodge. The best thing she could do now was keep busy. Preferably with something physical that would use up her nervous energy. She'd check with Dwayne and see what she could do. By the time Mack returned she'd have all these silly notions out of her head and her common sense would have returned.

She hoped. Thankfully, tomorrow night was the widow's meeting and she had several things she wanted to share with them. She prayed that with their combined wisdom and experience, they could help her navigate this maze of emotions.

Chapter Nine

Mack drove down the long and winding road that led to the lodge, soaking up the familiar landscape. It was good to be home. He was bone tired and in need of a day's rest and some good food.

Before all that, however, he needed to hold Lucy and let her know he was home for good. An image of holding Carly flashed through his mind, too. He'd welcome a hug from her. He'd welcome any chance to hold her close, which made him all kinds of a fool. They'd become close again, as friends. For him to think of anything more was pure nonsense. His feelings for Carly, as long held as they were, would never develop into a real relationship no matter how much he wished otherwise.

Pulling to a stop at the front of the lodge, he got out, receiving a warm welcome from Riley, who trotted alongside him to the porch. Mack stepped inside the lodge and was greeted by a loud squeal from Thelma, who hurried forward with her arms outstretched.

"Dear boy, we didn't think you'd ever get here. Are you all right? You know you scared us all half to death when we heard about the shootings."

He returned her hug. "Sorry about that. Things were a bit crazy."

"Daddy Mack!"

Lucy ran through the lobby and launched herself into his arms, hugging his neck with all her might. He held her close, not wanting to let go. His love for this child went deeper every day. "I missed you so much, sweetie."

"I missed you, too." She kissed his cheek three times. "And guess what. I have the perfect name for you. Daddy Mack. Isn't that good?"

He hugged her again. "I think that's a perfect idea."

Dwayne came forward, followed by Carly and Ella. His gaze locked with Carly's, but Dwayne stepped in front of him, blocking his view.

"Son, you are a sight for sore eyes. Glad you're home in one piece."

He clapped him on his right shoulder, causing Mack to wince and pull away. The look of concern on the older man's face touched Mack. "It's all right. Just a small graze. It'll heal in no time."

He glanced over Dwayne's shoulder and saw Carly had turned pale. He'd wanted to explain about his wound after things had calmed down. Ella hurried up to him, looking up at him with her big brown eyes bright and shiny. Eyes so much like her mom's.

"I'm glad you're home, Mr. Mack. I don't like it when you're not here. Lucy gets really sad and I do, too."

He lifted her up and gave her a kiss on her cheek. "I'm sad when I'm away from y'all, too. Thank you for welcoming me home, Ella."

Carly hung back until the others had moved off.

When she stood in front of him, he saw tears in her eyes.

"I thought you were dead."

"I'm fine. I couldn't get killed. I had to come back to my girls."

Carly flung her arms around his neck and held on for dear life. Holding him close, overwhelming him with a fierce tenderness and protectiveness he'd never experienced before, making it hard to breathe.

Carly slowly released her grip on his neck

and drew back, her own eyes searching his. Her hand trailed down his right arm. He knew she could feel his bandage beneath his shirt, and she'd realized his wound was more than a simple scratch.

"I'm glad you're back."

Her admission left him off-balance. He wanted to believe the sincerity and affection he saw in her eyes, but he didn't want to read too much into it, either. "You're just glad I'm here to help finish the repairs." He'd meant it as a jest, but Carly stepped back.

"You're right. That's all that matters."

She held his gaze a long moment and he realized he'd hurt her feelings. But he was afraid to believe that her words were more than normal concern for a friend. "Sorry. I shouldn't have been flippant. I'm tired. Thank you for caring. I mean it."

She nodded but didn't move, and he sensed she wanted to say more, but Lucy came up and took his hand. "Will you come play with me?"

How could he refuse such a request? He smiled at Carly. "I've been summoned." He walked off with Lucy, but he could feel Carly's gaze on his back. What did she want to say to him? Maybe when he had a moment he'd find her and see what he could coax out of her.

* * *

Carly pulled her sedan into a spot in front of the two-story office building in Hastings that housed the widow's group. Ashley met her at the front door. Once inside the elevator, Ashley touched her arm.

"Carly? Are you all right? You look tired."

Carly inhaled slowly, then nodded. "Just lost in thought, I guess."

"You must have been terrified not knowing if Mack was safe or not. When I saw that report on the news, I wanted to call you. I knew you'd be stressed, so I decided praying might be more productive."

"Thank you. I wasn't in any shape to talk to people. I felt so helpless, and the not knowing—that was the worst part. Troy's death was so sudden. One minute he was there and the next he was gone. But with Mack, the uncertainty, the sense of hanging in limbo waiting to hear if he was alive or…" The elevator opened and they stepped out. "I never want to go through that again. It was as bad as waiting for Ella to come out of surgery. Every moment felt like an eternity."

"You care for him a great deal, don't you?"

"I do. He's like family."

"Is that all?"

Carly didn't have an answer, at least one she was ready to share. Thankfully, they'd arrived at the therapist's office and Carly pulled open the door. Tonight she planned on simply listening to everyone else. Her mood had shifted and she wasn't ready to talk about her own problems.

After greeting all the women, Carly settled into her favorite chair and felt much of her tension start to ebb. Being around these ladies, knowing they understood, was a blessing that gave her great comfort. She allowed herself to become engrossed in each widow's comments, offering a nod of agreement now and then.

Until Trudy spoke. Like Carly, Trudy had lost her husband to a heart attack in her twenties. They'd only been married a year. Carly felt a deep connection with her experience.

Trudy twisted the edge of her sweater in her hands. "I need help. I've, uh, met someone and we've been going out. He's really nice and fun, but I..." She stopped and looked at Nina. "I don't know what to do. What should I do?"

Carly listened closely as each woman offered her advice, most of which encouraged Trudy to pursue the relationship with her new young man. But her concerns and reluctance were similar to Carly's. How did you let go and love someone else when you had loved your husband so completely?

Trudy posed the same question Carly had been wrestling with. If she was developing feelings for Mack, did that mean she hadn't loved Troy as much as she should have?

The two men were so different. Mack brought out the best in her. He made her challenge herself, forced her to be truthful with herself and pushed her out of her comfort zone. Troy had created a comfort zone around her, kept her protected, happy and comfortable. Together they had been a happy couple. Safe. Predictable. Warm. Until he died. Then her world had become cold and harsh.

The truth was she'd always loved Mack. And she was falling for him again. He was the standard by which she measured other men. Troy had come closest. He'd been kind, generous and loving. He'd treated her like a princess and he'd adored Ella. Being a father was his greatest joy. She had loved him, deeply. Had it been enough? Had she cheated him of her deepest love because she had given that part of her heart to Mack when she was young?

The meeting ended and Carly took her time gathering her things, hanging back, not wanting to make small talk this evening. She was the last to leave, but Nina stopped her in the reception area.

"I can see something is on your mind. Would you like to talk about it?"

Carly shook her head. "I need to sort it out on my own."

"If I had to guess, I'd say you and Trudy are facing the same dilemma. Am I right?"

Nina Johnson didn't miss a thing. Many times she'd helped one of the widows home in on a crucial problem and guided them through the shadows. Maybe Carly could benefit from a different point of view.

"I'm starting to have feelings for someone and I'm worried that... I mean, I loved my husband. I truly did, but what I'm feeling now is so much different, so much—"

"Stronger?"

She nodded.

Nina touched her arm gently. "I understand completely. When I met my current husband, I fought like crazy not to love him. My first husband was a wonderful, noble man, a chaplain who offered spiritual comfort to many. I thought if I fell in love with another man, I'd be dismissing our marriage as unimportant."

"How did you get over it?"

"I finally realized that there's no one way to love someone. My love for Chip was a totally different set of emotions from my love for Bret. I wasn't stealing something from the past and giving it to the present. It was simply a different man and a different kind of love."

"But I think I've loved this man since I was young. I'm afraid I've somehow cheated Troy because this other man still owned part of my heart."

"I understand, but a wise friend asked me a question when I was at the same point you are. She asked me if my husband loved me and if he would want me to honor his memory by being alone or to be happy and share the future with someone I loved."

Carly nodded. "Thank you, Nina. You've given me a lot to think about."

"I'm here whenever you need me. And remember. I'm a widow, too. I understand what you're going through."

After saying goodbye, Carly headed home, contemplating what Nina had said. If only she could flip a switch and turn off her emotions in one area and flip them on in another. Her biggest challenge now was keeping her feelings hidden from Mack. There were still too many obstacles between them to let her heart carry her away.

Mack strolled along the edge of the lake toward the worship center on the north side of the lodge. Thelma had told him Carly was working in the outdoor chapel this morning and he was hoping to have a word with her. She'd been avoiding him since his homecoming and he wanted to know why.

As he followed the path and made the curve to the center, he caught sight of her near the altar with its giant handmade cross, the centerpiece of the outdoor church. She looked adorable in her usual work attire—khaki cargo shorts, a blue tank top and sturdy boots. With the sunlight coming through the trees, he could imagine her as a teenager again, though he much preferred the grown woman Carly was now.

He slowly approached the altar, walking down the center aisle. "I'd forgotten how peaceful the place was."

Carly turned to face him, but made only brief eye contact. "It is. And, as far as I can tell, it's in good shape. I only found one loose bench."

"Good to hear."

Carly looked away, putting her tools back into her small toolbox. "How's your arm?"

He moved his forearm up and down. "Almost healed. It really was a minor wound."

"I'm glad. I was— We were all very concerned about you. We prayed for you every minute."

"And I felt that. I also felt you wanted to tell

me something that day I came home." He saw the reluctance in her expression and her refusal to look him in the eyes. "Anything happen while I was gone?"

She hesitated a moment. "I decided to take your advice."

"Oh? About what?"

"I tracked down the woman who left her earring in my dad's car."

"Really?" He hadn't expected that. "How did it go?"

Carly sat down on one of the wooden bench pews. "I found out that my mom lied about everything. She was the one having an affair, not my dad. She was planning to run away with a man named Richard, but he stood her up so she turned all her anger and humiliation onto my dad. We left the next day."

"I'm sorry."

She met his gaze. "I shouldn't have believed her, but everything she said made sense. Then I found the earring and it came right after Dad missed my birthday to be with you."

"I explained that."

"I know but it was all too much. I just wanted to get away from here and everyone connected with Longleaf. I felt like there was no reason for me to stay. I left and never intended to come back."

"But you did. The next summer."

"I had to. It was part of the custody agreement. I had to spend summers with my dad."

A rush of courage rose in his chest. "I was very glad you did. I didn't think I'd ever see you again. I was disappointed when you left after only a week." Carly's cheeks turned a light pink. Was she embarrassed by his admission or was there something else?

She stood and put some distance between them. "Well, I didn't want to stay any longer. It was clear I wasn't welcome."

Mack studied her a moment. Her posture said she was hurt, upset. "Why did you think that? I remember your father being happy as a kid that you were back at the lodge. And I was, too. I'd missed my friend."

"Friend. Yes, of course. So do you always kiss your friends?" Carly blanched and ran up the aisle in a rush.

Mack reached out for her arm to halt her. "Carly. I'm sorry, that was a mistake."

"You made that very clear."

He exhaled a tense breath, trying to ignore the accusing glare in her eyes. "That's not what I mean. Kissing you wasn't the mistake. The timing was."

"I don't understand."

"That summer it was so great to see you again, but you were running hot and cold. One day you were like your old self and the next you were freezing me out."

"It was a confusing time for me."

"I remember. I found you up at your favorite spot, the fallen tree overlooking the lake. You were crying. We talked about Atlanta and how you didn't like your mom's new boyfriend. You even admitted that you missed the lodge a little. You were torn between being with your mom and your reluctance to come back and live with your dad. You were so sad and lost and I wanted to comfort you somehow. Then you looked at me with those beautiful brown eyes, and I forgot everything else."

"So you kissed me out of pity?"

"Of course not, but I didn't want to give you the wrong idea."

"And what idea would that have been? That you cared?"

How did he explain without telling her how he'd felt? How did he explain that that kiss had rattled him to his core and he was still trying to make sense of it after all this time?

Carly's brown eyes sparked and she crossed her arms over her chest. "Let me get this straight. You cared so much that you ran to your old girlfriend Natalie? I saw you two kissing in the canoe the next morning. I got the message, Mack. Loud and clear." She made a checkmark gesture in the air. "Kiss Carly. Next up, Natalie."

"You know that's not what happened." Mack tried to find the words to explain his behavior. At the time, seeking out his old girlfriend seemed like a logical way to erase kissing Carly, by turning his attention to someone else. But it hadn't worked. Nothing could erase the profound effect of Carly's kiss. Telling her that now would be a huge mistake, not to mention sounding ridiculous. Her words finally registered. "Wait. Did you leave because you thought I was toying with you?"

"What else could I have thought?"

She walked out of the worship center, leaving him at a loss for words. Had Carly run away that summer because of that kiss? He'd expected her to be angry with him or even uncomfortable. He'd worried that she might tell her father, but from what she'd just said, she'd been hurt and disappointed. Was it possible she'd cared for him, too, back then?

He'd always believed that kiss had affected her, too, but he'd thought he was imagining it to soothe his conscience.

Now he began to wonder.

* * *

Carly sat on the wooden deck steps watching Ella and Lucy tossing a squeaky ball between Petunia and Poppy. The girls were wearing their matching outfits today and looked adorable. Riley came and rested his head on her knee in a shameless ploy to be petted.

Sundays were her realignment days. Attending Lakeside Church allowed her to take a step back and refocus on what was really important. It was also a brief respite from Mack. He and Lucy attended a different church with the Thompsons. The Thompsons usually visited Thelma's mother, who was in a local nursing home, after services, and Mack and Lucy always spent the day together.

She and Ella took advantage of the afternoons to explore the Lake Hope community.

But the day was waning and the evening was warm and balmy, perfect for a cookout. This was her favorite time of day, when they all came back together. They'd worked hard this week and made good progress. The deadline was only two weeks away and if the inspections were done on time, they'd be ahead of the game. They could open for business and satisfy the conditions of her father's will. But that still left the big question of what would come next. Sell out or stay and run the lodge and campgrounds?

She glanced up to see Mack coming toward the deck from the direction of the lake. He looked good in his dark jeans and a light plaid cotton shirt with the sleeves rolled up. The fading light made his dark hair appear coal black and drew attention to his eyes. She'd avoided him since their conversation in the worship center. Talking about that kiss long ago had only muddled her thoughts and her emotions. She was glad when he merely smiled at her and went to sit with Dwayne at the patio table on the deck.

Thelma strode onto the deck with the plate of hamburger patties ready to go on the grill. She set it on the side shelf, then cleared her throat and clasped her hands in front of her.

"We have a problem. I just got an email from the Magnolia House in Olive Branch. They were calling to confirm their stay this weekend."

Dwayne muttered under his breath. "I'd forgotten about them. What did you tell them?"

"Nothing. I didn't know what y'all wanted to do about it. They had no idea the lodge had closed or that Wade had passed away."

Carly stood and came to the table. "I don't understand. What's this about?"

Dwayne leaned his arms on the patio table. "A few years ago, your dad partnered with an orphanage up in Olive Branch to bring the children to the campgrounds for a weekend. It's their big trip each year."

Carly took a seat. There was no way they could host a group of kids. "Can't we reschedule?"

Mack crossed his arms over his chest. "How? We don't even know if the campgrounds will be operating in a few weeks."

Carly didn't appreciate his insinuation. "Then we'll have to cancel."

Dwayne stood. "No. This weekend was your dad's pet project. We need to find a way to make this happen. We can't disappoint those kids. It means the world to them." He glanced at his wife. "We've seen firsthand the joy on those kids' faces."

Mack nodded. "How many kids are you talking about?"

Thelma came to the table as Dwayne placed the burgers on the grill. "Ten to fifteen. They usually stay in the big cabin. We provide the meals and supervise the activities."

"The big cabin isn't nearly ready for guests and they're going to be here in six days."

"Five days. They always arrive on Friday afternoon and leave after breakfast on Sunday."

"How are we going to do this? We're not even sure we can get the place open before the deadline. Trying to open a week early is practically impossible."

Dwayne shook his head. "Nothing is impossible. We simply have to rethink things, that's all. Mack, how does our to-do list look right now?"

"I'll get my tablet and we can see where we stand." He went inside to retrieve his device.

Thelma drummed her fingers on her arm. "My biggest problem is staffing. I haven't hired nearly enough people to run the lodge, let alone a grounds crew. The children will want to swim, but the young man who will run the snack bar can't start for another week. Maybe I can get him to come for those few days. With extra pay."

Dwayne flipped the burgers, then closed the lid on the grill. "We can house them in the smaller cabins. Boys in one and girls in the other. The watercraft are ready."

"Since they're staying in the cabins, we don't need to worry about maids and I can handle the cooking for a group that size. The children tend to eat at the snack bar, and we always provide a cookout in one of the pavilions on Friday night."

"If we open for the group, how do we handle the others who've been wanting to make reservations?"

Thelma waved off the concern. "We'll call it a private party. We've hosted many in the past."

"So if we pull this off, will this private party qualify as the lodge being open? Will the conditions of the will be met?"

Mack rubbed his chin. "Good question."

Carly tucked her hair behind her ears. "I'll call the attorney first thing in the morning."

Dwayne adjusted his cap. "The biggest hurdles are the building inspections and the health department okay on the kitchen and the snack bar. Without those, we can't do anything."

Thelma turned worried eyes on her husband, then on Mack. "What do I tell the folks at Magnolia House?"

Dwayne stood. "Tell them we'll be looking forward to hosting them. I'm not going to disappoint those kids."

Carly could see how much it meant to the Thompsons. If it had meant that much to her dad, then she wanted to make the weekend work, no matter how much had to get done. "So where does that leave us repair-wise?"

Mack slipped his hands into his pockets.

"Clearing the trails, moving extra beds into the two smaller cabins and repairing the fishing dock."

An excited smile appeared on Thelma's face. "I'll take care of stocking the pantries. You three handle the rest."

Mack looked at Dwayne. "If you'll handle the dock repair, I'll finish painting the cabins."

Carly saw a hole in their plan. "But what about that weekend? If we're going to work with a skeleton crew, then we need to assign responsibilities."

"We'll do what we did back in the old days." Dwayne grinned. "I'll handle the watercraft. I'll get the old corn hole game set up, along with the badminton. I'll also double-check the playground. Thelma will be in charge of food and hostess duties—and the girls. Mack will handle the snack bar and pool. The kids always swim as a group, so that will be easy."

"What about me?" She didn't want to be left out.

"You'll do what you used to. Be the liaison between the leader of the group and us. Make sure they have everything they need and have a great time. You were always good with the guests, especially the little ones."

Carly rubbed her lower lip. "This all sounds good, but without the building inspections and the health department okay we can't do anything. Scheduling the inspections have been nearly impossible. They're overloaded to begin with and I've been unable to persuade them to move us ahead of the others. We can't do anything without those."

Dwayne tugged on his ear. "I think I can help with that. I know a few guys who owe me favors. Let me see what I can work out."

Thelma sighed. "I'll let the group know."

Dwayne scooped the burgers onto a large plate. "I suggest we enjoy this meal and the beautiful weather because we may not get another peaceful meal for the rest of the week."

Chapter Ten

The sun was climbing the treetops when Mack strode into the kitchen at the lodge the next morning. He'd slept longer than normal, which meant he was nearing the end of his physical limits. After the manhunt and learning that the Magnolia House children would be coming, he was worn thin.

Lucy trotted behind him, climbing up on a stool in the main kitchen. "I'm hungry."

Thelma chuckled and gave her a big hug and kiss. "I suspected as much. Would you like pancakes or French toast this morning?"

She thought a moment. "I think I'd better wait and see what Ella wants."

"Wants for what?"

Carly entered the kitchen holding Ella's hand. The child broke free and scrambled up on a stool next to Lucy.

Mack couldn't take his eyes off Carly, wondering if she always looked so adorable in the morning. The chambray shirt she wore over white shorts made her look like a breath of spring. Shoving that thought aside, he smiled and went to pour coffee into his travel mug.

"You're getting a late start today." She came to his side and poured a cup for herself.

"I'll make up for it by working twice as hard."

She chuckled. "I know you will. I remember how hard you worked. It was one of the things my dad admired most about you. He always knew you'd be a success at whatever you chose to do."

"I worked hard because I didn't want to let him down."

"You never did."

"Miss Thelma, Lucy and I decided we want French toast with orange juice, please."

"All righty. French toast it is."

Mack laughed. "Thelma, you have been bamboozled good. Those girls have you dancing on a string."

"I know it and I love it, so you hush."

Carly took a sip of her coffee. "Where are you heading first?"

"The Carly's Hill Trail. With all this rain we never did get it cleared out."

"Need any help?"

"Sure. I can always use a hand and the company."

They rode in silence to the trailhead. Mack steered the Gator onto the path, slowing to a crawl as he navigated the path. He stole a glance at his companion. Something was on her mind, and he debated whether to ask her about it or let it slide. He decided to try a nonpersonal topic. "I was sorry to hear that our private party doesn't qualify as the lodge being open."

"Me, too, but Mr. Holt pointed out that the deadline for being open to the public is only three days out from the weekend so technically we're ready."

Mack pulled to a halt and hopped out, hoisting a large twisted limb onto the trailer behind the four-wheel Gator while Carly gathered up a few branches and a fallen section of vine and tossed them deeper into the brush along the trail.

"Do you think we can get everything ready for the children this weekend?"

"I don't see why not. It's going to be a busy few days, though."

"I never expected my dad to get involved with orphans."

"Really? I think it was exactly something

he'd do. I told you how unhappy he was after you ran back to your mom's that summer. It was shortly after that when·he got involved with Magnolia House. I think it helped him cope."

"I guess I never really knew the man, only the father, and that was only a part of who he was."

A few yards farther on, Mack halted the vehicle and loaded more downed limbs onto the trailer while Carly cleared out the smaller debris. Having Carly working with him brought back fond memories of other tasks they had performed together. Every tree, leaf and stone here at the lodge held memories of Carly. It was as if she were a part of his DNA. He didn't want to think about how he'd get used to living without her again. He'd realized that more than anything, he wanted to make her happy. That meant agreeing to sell the campgrounds and letting it go to a stranger, no matter how much the thought tore at his heart.

Back in the Gator, he continued along the upward sloping trail until he felt Carly's gaze studying him.

"You're awfully quiet. Something on your mind?"

"You mean other than the kids coming and the hurricane in the Gulf?"

"It's still moving away from us, last I checked."

"That's a blessing." Carly fell silent again.

He wasn't ready to discuss the sale of Long-leaf so he brought up another topic that was weighing heavily on his mind.

"Val has asked me to adopt Lucy. She's willing to sign away her parental rights so I can become her legal parent. Val thinks she needs the stability I can give her as she grows up." He rubbed his forehead. "I love Lucy as if she were my own, but that feels wrong to me."

"I can understand why she'd want to do it, given her circumstances, but I can't imagine legally giving up my child. Have you decided what to do?"

Mack shook his head. "I wish your dad were here. He'd know exactly what I should do. He gave great advice. I relied on him a lot."

"I went to him about everything, too. Except the most important thing. I should have asked him about the affairs. At least let him tell his side of things."

Mack stopped the cart. "Do you really think you could have done that?"

"No, but I could have at least listened to his side of things. Just like I should have asked him about that day he forgot my birthday dinner. But I was too hurt and angry, and I didn't want to hear it."

Mack brought the Gator to a halt near the bench overlooking the lake. The one Wade had made for his daughter. Carly climbed out and approached the bench, letting her hands trail along the smooth back before taking a seat. Mack joined her, waiting silently, sensing a shift in her mood. He longed to pull her close and comfort her, but he doubted she'd allow that right now. Instead, he waited for her to share what she was thinking.

"I didn't think he even thought about me."

"He never stopped. You were his daughter. I think he got discouraged when you didn't answer his letters or emails." Carly faced him, a deep frown marring her pretty forehead.

"I never heard from him. I never received any letters. And as for emails I was online every day, I would have seen any messages from him."

"Would you have responded?"

"I don't know. Probably not at first."

"I think building this bench was his turning point. He was more like his old self after that, though a part of him was still missing."

Carly trailed her fingers along the arm of the wooden bench. "He was always ready to help others. I'm not surprised he got involved with the kids at Magnolia House."

"He was so excited when you married and had Ella."

"I can't believe Troy got in touch with him without telling me." She shook her head. "That's not completely true. We argued frequently about me ignoring my dad. Troy thought I was being too harsh."

She turned her back and brushed her fingers across her cheeks. Mack's heart went out to her. Facing the truth was never easy. He moved close and rested his hands on her shoulders, fully expecting her to pull away. Instead she leaned back against him.

"I've been so wrong about him, and now it's too late to let him know."

"He understood, Carly."

"How do you know that?"

"Because he loved you, no matter what came between you." He turned her around and pulled her close. "Don't ever doubt that. Your husband bridged the gap for you and it made Wade very happy."

"But it should have been my job to do that."

She looked up into his eyes. The sadness he saw there melted his heart. He brushed hair from her damp cheek, allowing his thumb to brush against her soft skin. He inhaled her sweet scent as she leaned toward him. His heart pounded fiercely in his chest with anticipation.

Suddenly Carly pulled back, a look of shock on her face. "No. We can't... I don't want..." She stood. "I'm going back to the lodge. I'm sure Thelma could use some help."

"I'll drive you back."

"No. That's silly. I can walk." She hurried off down the trail, leaving him more confused than ever. He was certain her feelings for him were as strong as his for her, but she was refusing to acknowledge them. He wanted to know why. There were too many options for him to pinpoint one. Was she afraid of commitment? Was it because of Ella and the large hospital debt? Or was it because of the will and the looming decision about the future of the campgrounds?

It was time to find some answers.

Carly stood at the edge of the deck staring out at the lake, but her mind was too troubled to appreciate the view. The children from Magnolia House were due to arrive late this afternoon and, thanks to a lot of hard work and many sincere prayers heavenward, everything was ready. There was only one giant obstacle to overcome. The health department inspections. Dwayne had managed to get the building inspections moved up, thanks to his longtime friendship with the inspectors. But the health department inspection had been rescheduled three times this week. If they didn't get the approval today they'd have to find other ways to provide food for the children. Thelma was working on alternative ideas. The biggest setback if they failed the inspection would be the inability to use the snack bar as the main food area.

A tapping behind her pulled her attention to the doors leading to the deck. Thelma stood there with a smile on her face giving her a thumbs-up sign. The inspector had arrived. Another prayer answered.

She caught sight of Mack as he drove past the lodge, and the memory of his comforting embrace warmed her. He'd almost kissed her again and this time she'd almost let him. Only the thought of the dictates of the will looming between them kept her from going through with it. Neither one of them knew what the future would be. Being at the lodge had done what everyone had hoped. It had forced her to remember how much she loved the place and her father.

Time here had revealed the truth about her parents and renewed her friendship with Mack. And her attraction. She was falling for him again, not with the shallow emotions of a young girl, but with the deep feelings of a woman.

There was no way she could allow those feelings to grow no matter how much she wanted to. Until the future was settled, there were boundaries they needed to keep. Once the Magnolia House kids left, they'd be officially open to the public for business. And they'd have to make a decision.

She could see herself staying here, running the lodge. Her online business was doing well. She'd taken on the Marina Fudge and Candy Shop as a new client, which brought her total client list to four. Back home Jessie was happy with her work and she wouldn't have to return to Atlanta.

But what would her life be like if she stayed at the lodge? Would Mack stay, too? Probably. His dream was to raise Lucy here at Longleaf. How could she deal with that? Would they be partners? Business associates? Or would he move back to the coast and raise Lucy there?

No time for this now. She had to focus on the weekend. Once that was over she could breathe a bit easier. The lodge would be open for business, hosting guests in a matter of days. The biggest question, however, still loomed.

Should she stay and run the lodge or sell out, pay off her debt and go home? The thought of returning to Atlanta didn't hold the same appeal as it did when she first arrived. She felt at home here. Ella was happy and they had family here.

Carly entered the lodge, making her way to the kitchen, where she found Thelma standing near the entrance, her eyes never leaving the inspector as he tested the temperature of the water, the refrigeration equipment and a long list of other things. She turned and left. This was Thelma's area of expertise. Nothing Carly could do to help.

There was plenty to keep her busy until the children arrived. Lucy and Ella hurried toward her from the back entrance. She could tell by the bright looks on their faces they had something up their sleeves.

Carly crossed her arms. "Okay, what are you up to?"

"We want to make the orphans happy to be here."

Lucy nodded in agreement. "We want to pick a bunch of flowers and put them in the cabins. Flowers always make people happy."

"Especially the gardenia ones. They smell so good." Lucy tilted her head and sighed.

"I think that's a very sweet idea. Let's go do that right now. We also have to put Poppy and

Petunia in the apartment. They'll have to stay inside most of the weekend."

Ella pouted and whined. "But they are so cute. The orphans will love them."

"Some children are allergic to dogs and some are afraid of them. To be safe, we'll keep the little dogs inside so no one gets hurt or upset."

"What about Riley? He's a big dog. He could scare someone."

"Riley is very well behaved and he will stay with Mr. Dwayne whenever he's outside. But Riley is a good watchdog and guard dog. He'll help keep the children safe."

The activity kept Carly occupied and her mind off the inspection. Lucy and Ella fussed over the flowers until they were perfect. She had to put the skids on their new idea to get every child a stuffed animal and a bag of candy. It warmed her heart, however, to see the girls so eager to give to the children.

Mack pulled up in the golf cart as they were finishing.

"Hi, Daddy Mack. We put flowers in the cabins to make the orphans happy."

"That was very nice of you. I'm sure they'll enjoy them." He looked at Carly, a half smile on his face. "Good news. The health department has given us an A. We're ready for business."

Carly exhaled a deep sigh. "What a relief."

"Agreed. You ladies need a ride back to the lodge?"

They climbed into the cart. Mack started forward at a slow pace. "I have more good news. Ronnie Baker, the college kid Thelma asked to fill in at the snack bar this weekend—he'll be here first thing in the morning."

"Wonderful. That will leave the rest of us to concentrate on the children. I want this to be a wonderful experience for them." Finally, everything was going in a positive direction.

The butterflies were in flight in her stomach as Carly anticipated the arrival of the children later that afternoon. Everything was ready. Thelma had baked plenty of cupcakes, cookies and other treats. The two cabins were clean and filled with bunk beds for the children to stay in.

The snack bar at the pool had been stocked and the water treated so that it was a sparkling crystal blue. Everything was prepared, and Carly had brainstormed all kinds of fun activities to do with the children. Even Ella and Lucy were looking forward to the guests. The children were a little older than the girls, but they were eager to play hostess and show the kids around the grounds.

Dwayne called from the front entrance. "They're here."

The faded gray van clanked to a halt, leaving her wondering how the dilapidated old vehicle had made it all the way down here from Olive Branch in the far northwest corner of the state. The door opened and a tall blonde woman stepped out. Carly's heart stopped. Natalie Reynolds. The woman she'd seen Mack kissing that summer and the reason she'd left Longleaf. A cold rush surged through her veins even as her throat tightened.

The woman's gaze landed on Mack. "Mack. I didn't expect to see you here. What a nice surprise."

Mack opened his arms. "Natalie. I didn't know you were involved with this organization."

She held his embrace a long moment, sending small flicks of heat along Carly's nerves. Suddenly her delight for the weekend lost its appeal. Seeing Mack and Natalie together would be impossible.

"I'm the director of Magnolia House. I approached Wade several years ago when I took over at the orphanage, and he was eager to help. We couldn't have held these weekends without him. Are you the manager of the lodge now?"

"No. Just one of the heirs."

"Oh? That sounds interesting. You'll have to fill me in. I was so sorry to hear about Wade's passing."

"Yes. It was a shock. Let's get y'all registered and then I'll show you to the cabins."

"I think I can find them. It's our fifth year here, you know."

"Oh, Natalie, I'd like to introduce you to Wade's daughter. Carly Hughes, this is Natalie Reynolds."

Carly pasted a smile on her face that she was sure looked totally insincere.

"I remember you," Natalie said, and smiled as she shook her hand. "Nice to see you again, Carly."

Carly nodded silently, not trusting her voice.

A broad-shouldered man emerged from the van and stepped toward Mack, extending his hand. Natalie had transferred her hug to Dwayne, then turned to the man.

"This is Jack Younger, the director of education for Magnolia House."

The chatter of children grew louder and Mack gestured toward the lodge. "We'd better hurry or your kiddos might burst out of the van."

"You're right. They're ready to expend some energy after the long three-and-a-half-hour ride."

After Natalie had signed the register, she and

Mack headed out to the van. Carly watched as Mack placed a hand on the small of Natalie's back, gently guiding her out. She spun around, unable to watch them together, and came face-to-face with Thelma and her expression of disapproval.

"Would you like to tell me what's got you so wound up?"

"Nothing."

"Oh? Then would you care to explain why you went from excited hostess to grim greeter in a flash?"

There was no use in trying to fool Thelma. She knew her too well. "Natalie used to be Mack's girlfriend. A long time ago." She hoped Thelma wouldn't press any further. She didn't want to relive her humiliation from that summer.

Thelma chuckled. "Well, it's about time."

"What?"

"That you're finally admitting you have romantic feelings for Mack. I always knew you did."

"No, I don't." The skeptical look on Thelma's face made Carly squirm.

"A woman doesn't usually experience jealousy when she doesn't care."

She patted her shoulder and headed toward the kitchen. Carly sighed and sank onto the leather sofa. Her fun weekend was suddenly a burden. Thelma was right; she did have feelings for Mack. She just wasn't ready to deal with them. But spending the next three days watching Mack and Natalie interact was going to be difficult. Thankfully, her schedule provided her plenty of activity apart from the two of them. She'd concentrate on her responsibilities and the children. That was all that mattered.

Everyone was so excited and happy, filled with anticipation for the weekend. She was the only one who felt sick to her stomach. If ever she needed a sign that she and Mack weren't mean for each other, Natalie's unexpected appearance had confirmed that.

It was going to be a long weekend.

Mack stood beside the bed as Carly tucked the girls in for the night. Lucy was spending the night with Ella, but both girls were so keyed up from all the excitement of the orphans' arrival he doubted they'd fall asleep quickly. Each time they looked at each other they burst into fits of giggles.

Carly kissed Ella good-night and Mack placed a kiss on Lucy's forehead. "You two had better settle down. There's a lot more fun coming tomorrow."

"We get to swim with all the kids."

"And go in the boats."

Carly turned out the light. "Now hush and go to sleep. You'll need all your energy for the pool."

Giggles and squeals was their only reply.

Mack followed Carly downstairs. "I think our girls are overtired."

"It's been a busy evening. Would you like some tea?"

"That would be nice." Mack took a seat on the sofa, his gaze taking in the cozy room.

What would it be like to come home to a wife and family each day? If it was a warm and welcoming place like Carly's, he doubted he would ever grow tired of it. There'd been only a few times in his life when home had felt like a haven. A few years spent with his mother after Val had moved away, and the short time he'd been engaged. His fiancée had owned a little cottage that had been a refuge at the end of the day. Until it wasn't.

Carly returned with his tea and handed it to him, then took a seat in the chair. He watched her a moment. She'd been unusually quiet since the children had arrived. But then they'd all been busy with the cookout and the campfire. He was glad Jack and Natalie were keeping up with the children, because there were too many and they were too energetic for him.

"I'm not sure who had more fun this evening, the children or our girls."

Our girls. Is that how she thought of Lucy and Ella? It sounded good to him. It would be so easy to think of the four of them as a family. "I agree. So far everything has been going well."

"Have you checked the weather lately? Has the hurricane moved off?"

"Not quite. It's still drifting northwest so all we should get is a shower here and there. I'll keep an eye on it. This early in the hurricane season you never know how those storms will react."

"Good. I'd hate to have the weekend ruined for the kids."

She toyed with her glass a moment. "I was surprised to see Natalie."

"Yes. I was, too. I had no idea she was part of Magnolia House."

"So you haven't seen her since that summer?"

Realization dawned. Carly was jealous. His heart skipped a beat. You weren't jealous of someone you didn't care for. "No. We never spoke after that day. We didn't really click. We had very different interests."

"She seemed very glad to see you again."

"It's always nice to see a friend you haven't seen in a while." He held her gaze, willing her to understand what he was really saying.

"Yes, it is."

His pulse raced with fresh hope. Maybe Carly had feelings for him, too. Come to think of it, Carly had been distant all day. He'd hardly seen her until the cookout, and then she'd not spoken a word to him. He hadn't thought too much about it until now, though he could see now that Carly was particularly standoffish whenever he and Natalie were together.

He took a sip of his tea. Maybe it was time to test the waters. "Natalie and Jack make a good couple, don't you think?"

Carly's head popped up, her brown eyes revealing her surprise. "I didn't know they were a couple."

"Really? It's not like you to miss something like that. Anyone can see they're crazy in love." He stood, stifling the smile on his lips. Carly did care. Now all he had to do was get her to admit it. But with the uncertainty of the lodge hanging between them, he wasn't in a position to explore their relationship. "It's going to be a busy day. I'd better turn in. Thanks for letting Lucy stay with you and Ella."

"Believe me, it's easier to handle them together than separately."

"Agreed. Good night, Carly. Sweet dreams." He held her gaze, pleased to see a faint pink tinge rise in her cheeks.

He left through the French doors leading to the deck, keenly aware of Carly watching him. His hope rose. As soon as the situation with the lodge was settled he'd have a long, personal talk with Carly.

First chance he got, he'd tell her of his decision to sell the lodge. He should have done that already. Then he'd admit that he'd always loved her and let the chips fall where they may. If it didn't work out, then perhaps the Lord must have a better plan in store for him.

Chapter Eleven

Carly scheduled a few tweets and a Facebook post on her laptop before taking a long sip of coffee. Last night had passed quickly, with a cookout at the pavilion near the playground and a campfire complete with s'mores and a sing-along thanks to Jack and his guitar. Natalie had been preoccupied with the children, making sure each of them was settled and happy. Everything had gone like clockwork, and she'd been reluctantly impressed with how skillfully Natalie handled the fifteen children in her care.

Today would be busy, as well.

Mack and Dwayne had taken the children fishing and boating first thing this morning. Ella and Lucy had been included in the expedition and both had been bubbling with excitement all morning.

Carly had taken advantage of the free time to catch up on her virtual-assistant business, which was growing faster than she'd expected. After lunch Carly and Mack would lead the group on a hike along one of the trails, followed by craft time at the pavilion; then the rest of the afternoon there would be swimming in the pool.

Work completed, Carly changed into comfortable shorts and a top and laced up her walking boots. The temperature was in the high eighties today so a walk in the woods would be welcome. She was looking forward to showing the children all the wonders of the woods and the creek. If she could ignite even one child with an appreciation for nature she'd be happy.

She was also eager to spend some time with Mack. They'd both been busy with the events and she wanted his take on how things were going. More to the point, she wanted him to herself for a short while.

Carly and the girls arrived at the trailhead later that morning to find the orphans all eager to go on the hike. The fishing and boating had done little to curb their energy. Lucy and Ella ran ahead to be with the kids. Mack and Natalie were standing a good distance away, their expressions indicating something wasn't right. She joined them. Mack approached Carly.

"We have a problem."

"What? Did something happen to the children? Has there been an accident?"

"No. It's the hurricane."

Carly frowned. "That's down on the coast and it's headed west. It shouldn't impact us at all."

"It changed course overnight. It's shifted back east and north. That puts us directly in the path of the outer bands of the storm."

Carly didn't have to ask what that meant. Living in south Mississippi, she'd seen her share of hurricanes. As dangerous as the center of the storm could be, the outer bands of wind could cause just as much havoc with the high bursts of wind and the spin-off tornadoes. The storm had put them in a precarious position now.

"When will the outer bands reach us?" Hopefully, the hurricane would either slow, start to weaken or, God willing, change directions again and spare them.

"According to the weather service, it'll be here overnight or early morning. No way of knowing for certain."

Natalie stepped forward. "I think maybe we

should cut the weekend short and head home with the children."

"I'm not sure that's a good idea," Mack said. "Evacuation orders have already been issued for Hastings and surrounding areas, which means the roads are going to be clogged. You might end up stuck on the highway when the storms roll over. It might be better to stay here and hunker down until it passes."

"Mack is right, Natalie," Carly chimed in. "We're safe here. The lodge has been through several hurricanes. One was a direct hit and we suffered only minor damage. The safety of the children is most important."

"I agree. And I'd hate to deprive the kids of the rest of the fun things they are looking for-ward to doing."

"No need for that. We can finish out the day and we'll move the kids into the lodge at bedtime."

Carly nodded. "We'll make it like a special surprise. I'd hate to have them upset about the storm."

Natalie smiled. "Thank you both. The chil-dren are having such a fun time. I'm glad I don't have to ruin it."

"In the meantime, I'll have Thelma get things ready at the lodge and keep an eye on the storm." He looked at Natalie. "Why don't you go with Carly on the hike? I need to check with Dwayne and see what we need to do to prepare the grounds for the storm. We'll need to pick up some plywood to cover some of the windows."

Carly made a head count of the children, then added Lucy and Ella to the total. All present and accounted for.

After giving the children instructions to remain on the path, not to run too far ahead and not to touch any plants unless they checked with Carly first, they started down the Piney Woods Trail. Carly had chosen this trail because it would be the most fun and the easiest to corral a bunch of rambunctious children. Natalie fell in step with Carly, making her a bit anxious.

"I have to admit I haven't been on these trails since—"

"Since you and Mack dated?" Carly could have kicked herself for the comment. She sounded childish and petty.

Natalie cocked her head and smiled. "If you count going out two times dating. He had other fish on the line."

What did she mean by that?

"Do you have a problem taking the children on the hike with me, Carly?"

Heat infused Carly's cheeks. She'd never

been very good at masking her emotions. "No, of course not. Why would I?"

"Maybe because you've been casting curious glances my way all weekend. I got the feeling you wanted to ask me something."

"No. Nothing at all." Her words were quickly followed with a request for forgiveness from the Lord.

Natalie grinned. "If you say so."

Carly started off by pointing out the Longleaf pine trees explaining the campgrounds were named after them, but it soon became evident that the kids were more interested in pointing out bugs and asking questions than listening to the usual spiel. It was just as well since her heart wasn't in it.

Natalie chuckled softly. "Don't feel badly. The kids have short attention spans. Some of them have never experienced the woods like this."

"I guess I take it for granted, having grown up here."

"I always envied you that."

"You did?"

"Sure. You had this whole campground to play in, you were so comfortable with the guests, and you had Mack hanging on your every word."

"No. That's not—"

"Carly, whatever happened between Mack and me years ago meant nothing. He was trying to be honorable and not cross any boundaries. But his feelings for you were clear to anyone who really looked. I never understood how you couldn't see it. Toby Cruise, get back here. Don't get so far ahead of the others." She turned to Carly. "And just for the record, I'm engaged to Jack, so you don't have to worry about anything starting up again between me and Mack."

Carly's conscience tugged. "I'm sorry, Natalie. I didn't mean to be so rude. I never understood what happened between you and Mack back then. Forgive me. It's a wonderful thing you're doing with Magnolia House."

"Don't apologize or explain. Maybe when this situation with the will is settled, you and Mack can be honest about your feelings. You belong together."

The talk with Natalie relieved many of Carly's concerns, but brought forth a few others. Was there something brewing between herself and Mack? Were they both too uncertain to admit it, or was it the will that was complicating their relationship?

She had found no suitable answer to that question by the end of the afternoon. It had made working with Natalie more comfortable.

They'd bonded over the crafts activity and got everyone fed at the snack bar and into the pool for the afternoon.

The skies had started to cloud over and the wind had swelled from time to time, which meant the hurricane was getting closer. So far it hadn't threatened any of the activities. Swim time would be ending shortly, then the kids would return to their cabins to roast hot dogs over fire and make s'mores again. Jack and Natalie had several games lined up for them to play, as well.

A sudden dark cloud obscured the sun. Carly looked skyward to see the unmistakable swirling clouds in the sky. The outer bands of the storm were arriving. As if reading her mind, Mack pulled up to the pool parking lot and hopped out. She could tell by the look on his face he wasn't bringing good news. He glanced at the sky as he drew near.

"What is it?"

Mack motioned for Natalie, who was sitting on the edge of the pool watching the kids, to join them.

"The storm has shifted again. And it's sped up. We're going to get the first hit in about two hours."

Natalie exchanged anxious looks with them.

"What does that mean?" A strong gust of wind swept across the area.

"I think we'd better get the kids settled in the lodge as quickly as possible. The rain could start at any time and they need to be indoors. Let's get the children out of the water and back to the cabins. Have them pack all their things and take them to the lodge."

Carly spoke up. "Have them bring their pillows and blankets from their beds. Thelma and I decided it would be best to keep all the children in the main room of the lodge. I think they'll feel better together than in separate rooms."

Natalie nodded, clearly anxious about the sudden shift in plans. "Yes. I agree."

"Mack, why don't you help Natalie with the kids and I'll work with Ronnie to close up the snack bar and close the hurricane shutters."

A gust of wind, stronger than the last, pushed through, underscoring the need to act quickly. Wind damage was always a threat, but it was the pop-up tornadoes in the outer bands that posed the biggest danger.

It was going to be a long night.

Carly stood at the back entrance to the lodge as the children trudged up onto the deck lugging their backpacks, blankets and pillows.

They appeared excited, as if they were going to take part in a great adventure. They weren't wrong, but it might not be the kind of adventure they were expecting. She directed the children toward the center of the large lobby, where furniture had been shoved back to allow the children to spread out on the floor near the fireplace and away from any windows.

Thelma settled the boys in one area, the girls in another. The chatter and laughter almost made Carly forget that there was a dangerous storm approaching. It was already getting dark outside and the wind whipped the trees in circles as the conflicting wind currents swept over them.

Ella and Lucy had begged to stay with the children, and since she and the other adults would likely be up all night on watch, they had agreed. The girls entered from the apartment with blankets and pillows, each hugging a favorite stuffed animal.

"Mommy, can Poppy and Petunia come in now? They'll be all alone in the storm."

"They'll be fine. I shut them in the bathroom with a warm blanket and some food and water. That's the safest place for them."

She'd just finished getting Ella and Lucy settled near the other girls when Mack entered the room and came toward her. "How's it going in here?"

"We're about settled down, though I don't think the kids are aware of what's ahead. What about you?"

Mack nodded, resting his hands on his hips. "We've done all we can. We boarded up the windows on your apartment and some of the ones in the lodge. Dwayne told me your dad had installed hurricane-resistant glass in the large window, so we should be okay since we're not taking a direct hit."

A rush of wind rattled the windows, causing a sudden silence among the children. Their eyes were wide and curious.

"Is it going to be a bad storm, Miss Natalie?" freckled-faced Cory asked, looking anxious.

She bent down and fussed with his covers and smiled. "Maybe, but we're all safe and sound in this nice big cabin, and Mr. Dwayne and Mr. Mack are here to protect us."

Thelma tapped on Mack's arm. "Why don't you give the children a little pep talk, just to make them feel better."

"Me? I don't know what to say."

"Of course you do. Let them know what's coming, what to expect—they won't be so anxious if they're prepared."

"She has a point." Carly held his gaze. "It's

obvious they look up to you and they know you're a deputy. What you say will carry a lot of weight."

Mack ran a hand along the side of his neck. "Okay, if you think it will help."

Natalie nodded. "Jack just checked the weather radio, and we're going to get the first wave any minute. None of these kids have ever been through a hurricane, so they need to know what to expect."

Mack picked his way through the sea of little kids and stood in front of the fireplace. "Okay, y'all, listen up. I want to tell you about things that might happen tonight."

"There's a big storm coming," Brandon, one of the more quiet children, commented.

"That's right, Brandon. But we're safe here in the lodge. This is a big old building with big old beams." He looked up at the ceiling. "See all those giant pieces of wood holding up the roof? Nothing can knock that down."

A little girl raised her hand. "Are you sure?"

Natalie stroked her head. "Yes, Angela. He's sure."

"You don't need to worry. We have everything we need to get through the storm right here. We have water and food and—"

Ella interrupted. "Miss Thelma made zillions of cupcakes."

A ripple of laughter and happy shouts filled the room. "We also have lights and heat. The lights might go out during the storm, but it's all right because we have a backup generator that will give us light. Does anybody have questions?"

"Will the water get into the lodge? Our old house flooded once and everything got wet."

"No, we're up high off the ground."

A loud rush of noise descended on the roof.

Little Cindy Davis hurried to Natalie's side and held on tightly. "What was that?"

Mack quickly reassured her. "That's the rain on the roof. It's going to rain really hard at times, then it'll stop and start up again. The wind will come and go, too, and it'll be loud and it might knock some limbs off the trees or maybe even knock down trees, but we're all safe in here."

Jack stepped forward. "And we're still going to have fun like we did last night, except we'll be inside instead of outside. I have my guitar so we can sing songs and tell stories. Then we'll go to sleep, and when we wake up, the storm will be gone and we'll head back home."

The speech appeared to calm the children, but each time the deluge of rain would pound on the roof or the wind would roar through the trees, the children grew quiet. A few grew tearful, but between Natalie, herself and Thelma, they kept everyone comforted and their minds occupied.

Dwayne quickly entered the room and motioned Carly and Mack aside. From the look on his face, he had bad news. Her heart skipped a beat.

"We need to be prepared. There's a band of storms due any minute that have some strong tornadoes embedded. It's heading right for Lake Hope."

Carly sent up a prayer, then hurried to Natalie to let her know the storm was going to become dangerous.

"Oh, dear. Some of the kids are already becoming frightened. The constant stopping and starting of the rain and wind is upsetting them."

"I know. That's the worst part of a hurricane. It seems to roar on forever."

Jack stepped in front of the fireplace with a reassuring smile on his face. "Boys and girls, I want to tell you that we just learned that the storm might get a bit louder. But, like Mr. Mack said, we're safe here so don't worry. We're all here to take care of you."

Brandon sat up and looked around. "Where's Willy and Todd? They're my blanket buddies.

They went to the bathroom a while ago and they ain't back yet."

Natalie's grabbed Jack's arm. "We have to find them. Where would they have gone?"

Carly and Mack headed down the hallway beside the office where the public restrooms were located. Mack searched the men's room. "They're not here."

Carly checked the office and the storage room in the kitchen, hoping they'd gone in search of more snacks, but didn't find them. "Where could they have gone?"

The wind howled and whistled from the end of the hall. The door to the side deck was ajar. Carly's heart stopped. "Oh, Mack, do you think they went outside?"

He hurried to the door and pushed it open. Carly stopped behind him, horrified at what she saw. The two boys were at the railing staring up at the sky, pointing and laughing. They had no idea what kind of danger they were in. A loose planter or a stray limb caught by the wind could become a deadly projectile.

"Boys, get back in here. Now!"

They turned at the sound of Mack's stern command. He took them both by the arms and marched them back inside. "What do you think you were doing? This is a deadly storm. It's nothing to play around with."

Todd pointed over his shoulder. "We saw a shark."

Mack blinked and looked at her. She shook her head and shrugged. "There are no sharks here, Todd."

Willy nodded. "Uh-huh. We saw it fall from the sky. A big black one."

Mack rubbed the bridge of his nose. "It was probably the limb off a tree. Sharks don't fall from the sky, fellas."

Two little heads nodded vigorously. "Uh-huh. We saw them in a movie. There were lots of them." Todd raised his hands and dropped them in demonstration. "Yeah, they wiggled and shot right out of the clouds. It was awesome."

Natalie had hurried forward and caught the tail end of the explanation. "Boys, go join the others. We'll talk later."

"They thought a falling limb was a shark?"

She rubbed her forehead. "I'm so sorry. They stumbled on that silly movie a while back and that's all they talk about."

Carly watched as Jack and Natalie had a long talk with the boys before sending them back to the group. The next wave of wind and water passed quickly, followed by a calm period. With the children all finally asleep, Carly caught a few hours herself only to be awakened with Mack's gentle touch on her arm. "What is it?"

"One more heavy band on the way."

She could tell instantly that this one was worse than the others. She could hear the roar of the wind and the crack of trees and limbs as they were snapped in two. Her throat tightened. She'd been through numerous hurricanes and their aftermath, but that didn't make a person immune to the fear, only more respectful. A loud noise shook the lodge. She gasped and looked to Mack for an explanation.

"I think we've taken a hit. A tree maybe. I'll go check." He returned with a grim look on his face. "A tree fell on the front porch. The whole east side is destroyed."

No sooner had he said that than the power went off. Thankfully, the generator kicked in, casting a faint but reassuring light around the lobby. A couple of the boys woke up, but Jack quickly reassured them, and they settled down and went back to sleep.

Carly took a seat in one of the large leather chairs in the corner. She'd not sleep anymore tonight. Praying for safety and a quick end to the storm seemed a better option.

Mack woke with a start. He'd drifted off sometime after the storm had passed through.

All told he was lucky if he had gotten two hours of sleep. Dawn was just beginning to lighten the sky as he surveyed the main room of the lodge. Little bumps of blankets littered the floor with a few heads and faces visible on pillows. Thankfully, the storms had blown through without any more serious damage to the lodge. Other than the damaged front porch, they had been well protected.

He stood and made his way quietly to the kitchen and made a quick pot of coffee. After lacing a cup for himself with a little sugar, he moved to the window, bracing himself for what he might see. They had been kept safe inside, but outside was a different situation. A knot formed in his stomach, knowing that the storm hadn't been as kind to the campgrounds.

His gaze scanned the area outside the window, tabulating the damage. Branches, leaves, and odds and ends were scattered over the sloping lawn. A thick tree limb lay across the dock. Carly's favorite swing beneath the live oak was hanging by one chain. The stone birdbath was toppled, along with the lamp beside the path.

He hated to think what he'd find once he stepped outside. Dwayne entered the kitchen from the back door and headed for the coffeepot.

"Oh, good. You made a pot. One of these days I need to learn how to do that."

"How's it look?"

Dwayne shook his head. "I've only looked around the lodge, but it's not good. There are a lot of downed trees blocking the driveway. I got the chain saws out. They're on the porch."

"Then we'd better get to work. I'm sure our guests will be eager to get on the road."

Mack picked up one of the chain saws and walked around to the front of the lodge with Dwayne, stopping in his tracks as he saw the damage to the porch was more extensive than he'd realized. Repairing the roof would take a lot of time. More time than the looming dead-line would allow.

Shoving that thought aside, he slid into the golf cart and headed down the driveway.

Dwayne steered around a few broken branches. "I hope you're in the mood to cut things up. It's a mess out here. It'll probably take us several hours to clear it out."

"Maybe the others will be up by then."

"We'll make a survey of the grounds as soon as the kids are gone. I've got to tell you I don't have a good feeling about what we'll find. I've only done a quick peek at things near the lodge and the drive. That storm was worse than we thought. I think we had a tornado touch down, maybe even two."

Mack met his friend's gaze, and he understood what he wasn't voicing. If things were as bad as feared, there would be no opening in three days for Longleaf Lodge. No opening meant putting the place up for auction. Mack set his jaw, refusing to let that thought take root right now.

By the time they'd cleared the driveway and returned to the lodge, the van was parked out front, and children were awake and finishing breakfast. Carly caught his gaze. She wanted to know the extent of the damage. He stepped to her side and spoke softly in her ear. "We'll check on things as soon as the guests leave." She nodded in understanding, but he knew she was as anxious as he was to learn what the storm had done.

Both their futures rested on the lodge opening.

Chapter Twelve

Carly waved at the children as they settled in their seats. Jack shook hands with Mack and Dwayne, raised his hand in a salute to her and Thelma, then hopped in the van and took his seat behind the wheel.

Natalie gave everyone a hug, then came to her.

"Carly, thank you for a wonderful weekend. The kids had a great time. Even the storm was an adventure. You made everyone feel safe and secure."

"You're welcome. I'm so sorry the storm ruined some of the activities."

"Nonsense. We'll be back next year. We all look forward to it."

Carly didn't mention that the lodge might not be around next year. Natalie gave her a quick hug, then whispered softly, "Don't let that man get away. He's a keeper."

Carly nodded. "I know."

She watched the van until it disappeared down the long driveway. Dwayne and Mack headed out to make their assessments of the damage on the grounds, and she was dreading the report. Back inside the lodge, she got the girls settled with a movie, then gathered up all the blankets and pillows while Thelma cleaned away the breakfast dishes. Almost by silent consent, neither of them wanted to talk. Carly suspected the older woman was as anxious about the damage report as she was.

Despite the chaos of the night, Carly had taken satisfaction from helping the children and keeping them calm and entertained during the height of the storms. She'd also accepted that her heart really did belong to Longleaf, and the idea of it being lost left a sharp pain in her heart.

Her anxiety mounted with each hour the men were gone. From what she could see from the deck of the lodge, the storm had wreaked havoc beyond what they expected. The front porch alone was a disaster. A forty-foot pine had crashed the corner and taken down most of the east side. Reconstructing it would take far longer than the few days they had.

Thelma hurried toward her from the registration desk. "They're back."

Together they moved to the end of the hall and waited for Mack and Dwayne.

Carly could tell by their grim expressions that she wasn't going to like what they had to report. "How bad is it?"

Dwayne leaned against the registration desk and gestured to Mack. "I'll let you deliver the bad news."

Mack exhaled a long sigh and rested his hands on his hips. "As expected, there are trees and limbs down everywhere. The cabins came through in good shape, but a tree fell on the vehicle shed and damaged the Gator. Not sure if it's salvageable or not. The campsites and RV pads are intact, but the south dock is gone." He held her gaze. "The worst damage was to the pool and the snack bar. The building took a big hit and the pool lost the diving board. It looks like we might have had a tornado touch down. Then there's the damage to the lodge porch."

A sinking sensation settled in the pit of Carly's stomach. "The deadline to be up and running is three days away. What are we going to do?"

"Nothing. There's no way we can make all the repairs in time."

Dwayne removed his ball cap and placed it

on the counter. "We found out that the hotel resort took a bigger hit than we did. They'll be closed for several months."

"Are you sure we can't get enough things repaired to open in time? If the cabins and campsites are all right, then we'll just close the lodge. We still have the watercraft and the trails, so we could operate on a partially open basis."

Mack shook his head. "Without the snack bar the campers won't have a place to eat."

Carly rubbed her temple. "Then there's the safety factor. The trails are full of downed trees. I haven't even checked the trees that are partially down or damaged. We can't let folks walk those trails if a tree is suddenly going to give way."

"There must be something we can do. I'll talk to Mr. Hart first thing in the morning. There might be an act of God clause or something. Or maybe a loophole. None of this was our fault."

Mack crossed his arms over his chest, his gaze filled with sympathetic understanding. "I suppose it couldn't hurt, but don't get your hopes up."

"We have to do something or else..." She couldn't bring herself to say the words. She looked at the others, and one by one she saw the same defeated expression on their faces. No one wanted to voice the inevitable.

Auction.

Carly's stomach curled into a painful knot. Pivoting on her heel, she strode out of the lodge onto the deck and across the lawn, battling tears and anger and remorse. If only she could run away and avoid all of this. She stopped at the swing, heartbroken to find it hanging by only one chain. It was the last straw. Tears flowed down her cheeks. *Lord, what am I supposed to do now?*

"I'll get it fixed. I just need a ladder to put the chain on the hook. It's not damaged."

The sound of Mack's soft, low voice wrapped around her like a hug. She wanted to take refuge in his embrace, but that was out of the question.

"Are you all right?"

She crossed her arms over her chest and stared out at the water. Leaves and small branches floated on the surface, the grass below her feet was thick with pine needles and acorns ripped from the trees, and the air was thick with the scent of fresh pine. "I don't know. I never thought it would come down to the auction, Mack. I don't want to lose the lodge."

"Do you really mean that?"

Tears flowed. She nodded. "But now it's too late. There's no way we can make the repairs and be up and running in time. Longleaf will go to auction. Everything my dad worked so hard for all these years will be gone. I'm sorry, Mack. You tried to tell me, tried to make me remember what this place meant to me, but I was too angry to hear you."

"Maybe we should have sold out when you wanted to. At least then you could have gone home with the money to pay off the medical bills."

"This is my home."

Mack reached out and took her hand, pulling her close in his arms. "I never thought I'd hear you say that again."

"Me, either." She glanced toward the woods on the east side of the lodge. "Have you checked the worship center yet?"

"No. Let's take a look."

They walked slowly, holding hands. A sense of peace settled on her shoulders and dispelled her earlier despair. "I'm sorry, Mack. If I hadn't been so stubborn and childish, we might have been able to work something out."

"Does this change of heart mean you want to remain at Longleaf, run it, and raise Ella here?"

"I haven't thought that far ahead. I just don't

want to see the lodge dozed for a sleek hotel and the trails leveled for a golf course. Who knows what the next owner will do?"

They stepped through the trees into the clearing that held the worship center. "Oh, look. It hasn't been touched." The large cross stood firm and erect; the rows of benches were sound and solid. The sight opened a long-locked door inside her. All the destruction, the damage and the threat of losing her family heritage faded slightly as she looked at the outdoor sanctuary. God's house wasn't touched. It had stood strong throughout the raging winds and torrential rains.

She moved toward the front, taking a seat on one of the wooden bench pews.

Mack set his hands on his hips. "Can you believe this? The Lord must have had his hands covering this place."

"I always imagined I'd be married right here. Growing up, we held Sunday services regularly. I was going to have two white wheelbarrows behind the cross filled with blue and yellow flowers."

"Wheelbarrows, huh?"

She smiled. "It sounded romantic at the time. My mom used to paint our old wheelbarrows and fill them with flowers. It was so pretty." She glanced back at the pulpit. "There'd be a white wreath of roses on the cross and white cushions on all the pews. Two large gold candle stands on the podium. And candle stakes at the end of each row with white tulle and ribbon streamers. My twelve bridesmaids would wear blue dresses and carry yellow daisies."

"Twelve?"

Carly laughed. "I know. It's overkill, but at the time I wanted to include all my best friends."

"And what about you? What would you be wearing?"

"A white princess-style dress, simple and elegant, with a bouquet of white magnolia blossoms."

She fell silent, flooded with childhood memories that had been buried too long and the dreams that would, now, never be. "Ella could have been married here."

Mack took her hand. "What brought about this change of heart? All this time, you've dug in your heels."

"I've discovered that things I believed, that I accepted as truth, weren't true at all."

Mack held her hand, his thumb rubbing across her skin in a slow soothing rhythm, encouraging her to go on. "That little lies can lead to big problems, that even a small twist on the truth can ripple on forever. Things aren't always what they appear to be and we shouldn't just accept them. We need to ask questions. I just listened to what I was told and believed it as gospel, and it ruined my life."

"I agree. We need to be honest with those we care about. Tell them how we really feel because they can't read our minds. We can't just make assumptions on what we see or what we're told, because we don't always know the whole story. I don't want to live like that. It can hurt too many people."

Was he trying to tell her something? What unspoken truths were there between them? "I should have believed you when you told me my dad wouldn't cheat on my mom. Deep down, I think I knew that, but I couldn't get past the hurt."

"Another one of those distorted truths that have caused so much trouble."

"Exactly."

Carly inhaled a slow breath. "In the interest of honesty and openness, I need to tell you something. I came back that last summer because of you. I wanted to see you again. I missed you."

"You did? You never said anything."

"We had a good time that first week. It was like we'd never been apart. And then…"

Mack exhaled and nodded. "And then I blew it by kissing you."

Carly tried to hide her hurt. "Just what every girl wants to hear."

"I didn't mean it like that." He stared at the lake a long moment. "I'd wanted to kiss you for a long time. But I didn't want to cross any barriers and I wasn't sure how you would feel about it."

"What barriers?"

"Carly, you were my boss's daughter. Not to mention underage."

"That shouldn't have mattered. Besides, I would have been eighteen in a week."

"But you weren't, and it mattered to me, because I owed your father so much. He was my mentor and the father I never had. I wasn't going to jeopardize our relationship by taking liberties with his only child."

"But he adored you. He probably wouldn't have cared."

"Did you ever ask him?"

"Well, no, but…"

"So why did you kiss me? Just to satisfy your curiosity?"

"Partly. But more so because I'd had a crush on you from the moment I met you. When I was twelve."

"You had a crush on me that long?"

"More than a crush, actually. But you kissed me, then ran back to Natalie. I saw you both in the canoe the next morning."

"That was a mistake. I was trying to forget the kiss."

"Again. Thanks a heap."

Mack took her hand. "I didn't regret it. But I was trying to put it behind me, and I thought if I spent time with Natalie I could forget, plus I didn't want to risk upsetting you or your dad."

"Why would I be upset?"

"You have to admit, ours was a love-hate relationship. There were times when I thought you couldn't stand me."

"There were. I resented the close relationship between you and my daddy. I felt left out."

"Daddy? That's the first time you've called him that since you've been back."

"I miss him. He'd be so upset by all this damage."

"He would, but he'd dig in his heels and put it all back together."

"But I can't. And it's all my fault."

"No. We've both been stubborn. This is a poor time to tell you this, but I had decided to agree to sell the property."

"Why? I thought you wanted to raise Lucy here to run the lodge and give her a home?"

"I do. I did, but I realized I was being selfish. Wade was your dad. Not mine. No matter how much I loved him and the campgrounds, this is your family legacy. Not mine. I should never have gone against your wishes."

"But he left Longleaf to both of us. Though I'm not sure why."

"I think he hoped we'd be partners and run the campgrounds together. That would have made him happy."

"I suppose we'll never know for certain."

"Let's not give up until you talk to the attorney tomorrow. There might be a silver lining behind this black cloud."

Carly smiled up at him. "I'd forgotten how optimistic you can be."

"That's not optimism, that's avoidance. I don't want to think all is lost until I have to."

Carly slipped her hand in his as they walked back to the lodge. The connection helped her block out the debris and destruction all around them. He'd always made her see the good in everything. Much the same way her father had. Maybe that was why she loved him.

She stole a glance. Should she tell him? Or was this one of those secrets she should keep to herself? For now she'd have to wait and see.

Mack steered his SUV down the long winding driveway of the Longleaf Lodge and

Campgrounds a few days later, wondering if this would be one of the last times he took this journey. He glanced over at Carly, who was sitting slumped in the passenger seat staring out the window. She'd been unusually quiet and reflective since yesterday. He couldn't blame her. He felt like he'd taken a sledgehammer to the chest. He wished he had something hopeful to say to her, but the bottom line was the lodge was going up for auction today in less than an hour. They'd decided to wait it out by taking the girls to the marina and letting them play and have lunch to keep them distracted. Neither of them had any idea how they would tell their daughters why they wouldn't be able to visit the lodge anymore.

Mack reached over and squeezed her hand. "You did all you could. If there'd been a way out of this, Holt would have found it."

"I know. But I could have avoided all of this if I'd been honest with myself. Instead, I've wasted time and now I've lost everything."

"I'm not blameless, either. I should have sided with you sooner."

"Blaming ourselves won't help now."

Mack's chest tightened. With every moment that passed he realized more and more what he'd lost. Not only the dream of a home for Lucy, but his relationship with Carly. With the lodge gone, she'd have no reason to stay in Lake Hope and he'd never see her again.

Maybe it was time to start thinking about the next phase of his life. One that didn't include Carly and Ella.

The marina restaurant wasn't crowded, so they took a table near the beach playground so they could talk and watch while the girls played. Mack ordered burgers and fries, but only the children seemed able to enjoy them. The food turned to dust in his mouth and Carly must have felt the same way. She toyed with her fries, twirling one around in the ketchup cup a long while before taking a bite.

She met his gaze, and the pain and sadness in her brown eyes broke his heart.

"Funny how good news and bad news seem to go hand in hand."

"Meaning?"

"I heard from the medical assistance organization my friend told me about and they've accepted my application. They'll start working on my case immediately. I can stop worrying about the hospital bills, but now I have to face the loss of the lodge." She exhaled a heavy sigh. "This will be the longest afternoon of my life. No. I take that back. Waiting for Ella to come through surgery was the longest. But this runs a close second."

"Standing at the front of the church waiting for a bride who never showed up."

Carly jerked her head up. "What do you mean?"

"She changed her mind."

"You never told me you were engaged."

She squeezed his hand. "I'm sorry, Mack. That must have been hard."

"Not as hard as waiting on your child to come through heart surgery."

"Apples and oranges. Did she tell you why?"

Mack grinned. "She said that my heart was never fully hers. That I loved someone else who I couldn't get out of my system and she didn't want to be my consolation prize."

"Oh. Was she right?"

He rubbed his thumb over her finger. "She was."

"So why didn't you marry the other woman?"

"She was already married and I hadn't seen her in a very long time." He looked into her eyes, and he could see questions forming. Maybe now was the time to tell her everything. He had nothing to lose. Everything he'd hoped for was over. At least he could finally admit his feelings. If she didn't feel the same, it no longer mattered. After today they would probably go their separate ways.

"I never thought of you as the dating-a-married-woman type."

"We never dated. We only kissed once. But my fiancée was right. I'd given this woman my heart, and it was impossible to give it to someone else."

Carly's eyes widened and her cheeks blushed pink.

"I couldn't marry her because she wasn't you. I lost my heart to you, Carly, from the first moment I met you. I was fourteen and you were twelve but you were so feisty and funny and strong and smart. I didn't realize it was love until we were much older, but I knew no other girl ever made me feel the way you did. That kiss was the benchmark that I judged every other woman by. When you came back here, I knew nothing had changed. I love you, Carly. I always have. I'm sorry if it makes you feel uncomfortable or if you're troubled by my admission. But we may never see each other again and I wanted you to know how I felt. Have *always* felt."

He braced himself for her rejection.

"Mack. I wish I would have known sooner. We've wasted so much time." She reached out and touched the side of his face. "I've tried to deny it most of my life, but I love you, too. I think I have since the first day you came to work for us at the lodge. I was too young to understand what my feelings were, but when I came back the last time, it was clear to me. But I was too afraid to hope."

His heart took wings, afraid to believe what she was saying. He drew her close and kissed her. "Carly, I—"

Her text tone shattered the moment.

She blinked as if coming out of a daze. He knew the feeling. She looked at the screen. "It's Dwayne. The auction is over. We need to go back."

His joy over Carly's admission was replaced with the dread of learning the fate of the lodge. Neither of them spoke as they drove home. He couldn't remember a time when his emotions had soared and crashed in such a short span of time.

He didn't want to think about what tomorrow would bring. The lodge was gone. They would go their separate ways. Were their admissions of love enough to change the future or only a sweet moment in time, never to be mentioned again?

Carly fought the heavy weight of sadness that was lodged in her chest. Her gaze took in the lush surroundings outside the car window as Mack turned into the driveway at the lodge.

This could be the last time she'd see the land her family had owned for three generations.

She tried not to think about the new owners and their plans for the grounds. She glanced over at Mack. Was he feeling the same? They should have tried harder to work together. "What are you going to do now?"

"Go back down to Gulfport, I suppose. I have my job and an apartment. I think I might study for the bar exam. It would be a safer profession than being a deputy."

"I thought you loved law enforcement."

"I do. But I have to think of Lucy. What about you? What will you do now?"

"I guess we'll return to Atlanta. I still have a job, and I can keep promoting the marina stores on social media from anywhere."

"Is that what you really want to do?"

She didn't answer. What she wanted to do was stay here and run the lodge like her father wanted. Ella deserved the kind of childhood she'd had growing up, playing among the trees and beside the beautiful lake. Here she'd have the freedom to explore and thrive. Ella would learn about the family business, and eventually she'd take over some of the tasks Carly had done growing up. But that dream was dead now. Her throat tightened and tears stung her eyes.

Mack stopped the car in front of the lodge but didn't move. He met her gaze and a link of understanding passed between them. Neither of them was looking forward to hearing the fate of Longleaf Lodge. But they had to face the hard truth that each of them had contributed to this disaster. Pride. Anger. Self-interest and misunderstanding had brought them to this point.

Carly opened the door and got out, opening the back door for the girls.

"Can we play on the swing set?"

"No. Not yet. We need to see if it's safe after the storm. Why don't you find a movie to watch. There's still too much debris for you to play outside right now."

Mack came around the vehicle and held out his hand. She took hold of it, feeling her courage lift. They walked toward the entrance and climbed the porch steps slowly, as if approaching the guillotine. He stopped at the door and faced her. She searched his face, noticing how his blue eyes had faded to gray. She wanted to comfort him somehow, but there was nothing she could say.

He took her other hand in his and met her gaze. "Did you mean what you said at the marina? About loving me?"

"Yes. With all my heart."

"Then stay here with me. We'll build a new future together. The lodge might be gone, but that doesn't mean we have to part ways. I've lost you twice. I don't want to lose you again."

"What are you saying?"

"I love you. I love Ella. I want you both in my life forever. We can move to the coast. I'll get a bigger apartment or we'll find a house. Or, if you want, I'll come to Atlanta. I can always join one of the law enforcement departments there."

"Was that a proposal?"

"Yes. I've waited a lifetime to ask you. There's never been anyone else for me but you. You're the dream I've held in my heart since I was fourteen."

She smiled up at him, her senses overcome with her deep love for this wonderful man. "Yes, yes. I want nothing more than to be your wife."

He pulled her into his arms, his blue eyes revealing the depth of his love. His lips captured hers tenderly. Carly floated on the joy of his kiss and the knowledge that at long last the barriers between them had been removed. Mack ended the kiss and she rested her head on his chest, reluctant to let the moment end. But they still had to learn the fate of Longleaf Lodge.

Mack released her, cradling her face in his strong hands. "No matter what happens, no matter the fate of the lodge, we'll have the most important thing in life. Each other."

She nodded and slipped her arm around his waist. "I guess we'd better get this over with. Then we can start making plans for the future."

Mack opened the door and they stepped into the lodge. Dwayne called to them from the office. He was seated behind the desk with an unreadable expression on his weathered face. An unusual thing for him. His feelings were usually clearly visible and readable.

"Have a seat."

Mack and Carly sat, keeping their eyes on the man. Thelma moved to his side, an odd expression her face, as well. The extended silence was making Carly anxious. "Well? How did it go? Who bought the property? Will they keep it as is or are they going to—" Her throat seized up. "Are they going to tear it down?"

"No. The new owner isn't going to change anything. It'll all remain exactly as it always has."

Carly exchanged a surprised look with Mack. "Really?"

"Who bought it?"

Thelma laid a hand on Dwayne's shoulder and smiled. Carly studied them both.

They looked happy, almost mischievous. "I don't understand."

Dwayne leaned back in the chair, resting his hand on top of his wife's. "*We're* the new owners of the lodge."

His statement refused to register in her mind. "What are you talking about?"

Mack seemed equally confused. "Dwayne, you're not making sense."

"I couldn't let my friend's family legacy be auctioned off to strangers. Who knew what they'd do to the place? So Thelma and I talked it over and we decided we'd step in and bid on it. And we won."

Carly glanced between the two old friends. "But how can you afford it? I know what the place is worth, and it's more than the three of us put together could afford."

Dwayne chuckled. "Well, I happened to own a piece of land up north near Tupelo and it keeps spitting out oil. Thelma and I don't really have anything to spend it all on so we just let it accumulate in the bank. The lodge seemed like a good investment for our future."

Her hopes began to soar even as she was afraid to believe what she was hearing.

Mack smiled. "What *are* your plans for the future? Do you need a good manager? Someone who knows the place inside and out?"

"Or maybe an office worker who's familiar with the business?" Carly held her breath.

"Nope. Not going to need any help in that department, because I'm not keeping the place. I'm selling it."

Carly's hopes burst like a party balloon, leaving her confused and hopeless. "Selling it? Why? I mean, who are you going to sell it to?"

"You two."

"What?"

Mack leaned forward. "Dwayne, you know neither of us has that kind of money."

Dwayne grinned. "Sure you do. I've priced the place real reasonable. I even have the papers being drawn up. Provided you agree to the terms."

Mack scratched his jaw. "What kind of terms?"

Thelma patted her husband's shoulder. "Stop teasing."

"If you're agreeable, I'll sell the lodge back to you both for a dollar apiece. My only conditions are that Thelma and I continue to live and work here. Nothing will change, but you both have to stay and run the place. I want my friend's legacy to continue. Do you think you can do that?"

Carly reached over and took Mack's hand.

"Yes. We can. We both regret allowing the lodge to go to auction."

"It means working together. Closely." Dwayne looked at them with a strange expression.

"We know."

"Your daddy loved you both. He knew what was happening between you, but he didn't feel it was his place to say so. He figured you'd work it out in time. But then your mama left and, after that, things got complicated. I don't know for sure, but I suspect that Wade set his will up so you two would have to finally deal with all those unresolved issues. Have you?"

Carly exchanged smiles with Mack. "We have. It's taken us a while, but we finally admitted that—"

"We love each other."

"And what are you going to do about that?"

"We're getting married."

"About time. Well, you can work out the wedding plans later. We have a lot of repairs to make to get this place running again." He stood and took hold of his wife's hand. "I'll let you know when the paperwork is ready." He winked and closed the door behind him.

Carly shook her head. "I can't believe this. I thought the lodge was lost forever and now…"

Mack stood and pulled her close. She

wrapped her arms around his neck and held on tight. "It's ours. We can stay here and raise the girls and make the lodge everything we dreamed it could be."

He kissed her. "Our dreams are finally coming true."

Epilogue

Three months later

Carly slipped out of the dining room of the lodge and moved to the railing on the deck, inhaling the sweet scent of pine made sweeter by knowing the campgrounds were in the family once again. Her heart overflowed with love and gratitude, and she offered up a thankful prayer to the Lord.

Today had been the wedding of her dreams. She and Mack had exchanged their vows in the outdoor worship center. The day had been everything she'd imagined. She'd walked down the aisle behind Ella and Lucy as her flower girls. They'd looked adorable in matching white dresses with light blue sashes and sprigs of flowers in their hair. Ashley had served as her maid of honor, and Dwayne had stood up for Mack.

Her mother and stepfather had attended. Things between her and her mother weren't perfect, but they were making progress.

A wreath of white roses hung on the large wooden cross at the pulpit. Two white wheelbarrows filled with white flowers stood behind. Dozens of hanging baskets with white flowers hung from the trees. The guests had been seated on comfy white cushions.

The reception was held in the lodge dining room and Thelma had outdone herself with the decorations. Carly heard the lodge door open and smiled as she saw her new husband coming toward her. He looked impressive in his tux, even more so than his uniform. He stood behind her, slipping his arms around her waist. "Are you hiding out here or just enjoying the fresh air?"

"A little of both. I wanted to soak in the happiness. It's almost more than I can bear."

"I have to admit I want to pinch myself to make sure I'm not dreaming." He kissed her temple. "Was the wedding everything you hoped? Even the wheelbarrows?"

She giggled and nudged him with her elbow. "Yes, even the wheelbarrows."

"I have to admit, Mrs. Bridges, they looked better than I expected."

Carly snuggled against him.

The door opened again, and Lucy and Ella hurried toward them, the two puppies, wearing fancy bows around their necks, trotting alongside.

"Daddy Mack, now that you're married, does this mean Ella and I are sisters?"

Mack nodded. "I suppose it does. You're sisters by love."

The girls exchanged squeals and held hands.

Ella looked up at Mack. "Can I call you Daddy now?"

Mack hugged the girl to his side. "You can call me whatever you like because I love you both. And I love your mother. We're going to be the best family ever."

Lucy looked up at Carly. "Can I call you Mama?"

She exchanged a look with Mack. "Is that what you'd like to call me?"

She nodded. "I asked my mom and she said she didn't mind 'cause it's a blessing to have two mamas that love me."

Carly hugged her close. "I'd be very happy for you to call me Mama."

Ella turned to Lucy. "Maybe we can call

Miss Thelma and Mr. Dwayne Grandma and Grandpa now. Let's go ask."

They darted off, the doggies scampering close behind.

Mack slipped his arm around Carly. "I think we have us a very unconventional family here, my love. A dad who is really an uncle, sisters who aren't related, a stepmom who is more like a mom and two good friends who have been elevated to grandparents."

Carly looked out at the lake she'd loved all her life. "I feel so blessed I think my heart will explode. I'm in awe of how the Lord worked this all out. I didn't see any solution to the lodge or us, and now we're looking at a bright new future."

Mack kissed her temple. "Your dad used to tell me that no matter the size of the problem, love was always the answer."

She smiled up at her husband. "I think my dad was a very wise man."

* * * * *

*If you loved this tale of sweet romance,
pick up the other books
in the Mississippi Hearts series
from author Lorraine Beatty.*

**Her Fresh Start Family
Their Family Legacy**

Available now from Love Inspired!

*Find more great reads at
www.LoveInspired.com*

Dear Reader,

Welcome back to Hastings, Mississippi, and the ladies of the widow's walk group. I hope you're enjoying reading about the widows learning to love again after loss. I have a lot of admiration for the women who are courageous and carry on. Carly is one such woman. Life has given her many challenges and she's strived to rise to the cause. But many of her issues are things she needs to confront.

The words of one of my favorite hymns kept repeating in my mind as I wrote this book. *"Oh what peace we often forfeit, oh what needless pain we bear. All because we do not carry everything to God in prayer."*

Have you ever taken something at face value because you didn't want to know the truth? Had you sided with someone because you were loyal, never asking what actually happened or because you were unwilling to accept that the person you cared about would shift the facts?

Mack and Carly learned the hard way how much jumping to conclusions can distort a relationship far into the future.

Sometimes we have to stop and face the truth, ask the hard questions and stop accepting the standard explanation. It was only when

Carly and Mack let go of the old notions and half-truths, and allowed the Lord to shine a light on the truth, that they were they able to put the past behind them and embrace the future they were supposed to have.

I hope you'll enjoy their journey as they travel the winding road to their happily-ever-after.

I love to hear from my readers. Contact me on my website or through Love Inspired books or directly at Lorrainebeatty@comcast.net.

Blessings,
Lorraine

Get 4 FREE REWARDS!

We'll send you 2 FREE Books <u>plus</u> 2 FREE Mystery Gifts.

Harlequin® Heartwarming™ Larger-Print books feature traditional values of home, family, community and—most of all—love.

FREE
Value Over
$20
